W9-CFJ-995

Out Of Control.

"I always liked a good fight, Kat," J.D. said.

"And I'll tear you apart." She breathed shakily, lifting her head slightly as though she regretted giving him an inch. The gold flecks in her eyes caught the light and shimmered with anger.

"Really?" he drawled, smiling slightly. "My knees are shaking now."

Kat's long, elegant nails sank into her briefcase. "They should be."

The pulse at the base of her neck beat against the expensive, creamy material of her blouse, and J.D. allowed himself to gaze lower. It was all there beneath the long strand of perfectly matched pearls—the slender softness, the woman she chose to hide beneath the fashionable suit. He could see her sigh, feel her ebbing control....

Dear Reader:

Welcome to the world of Silhouette Desire. Join me as we travel to a land of incredible passion and tantalizing romance—a place where dreams can, and do, come true.

When I read a Silhouette Desire, I sometimes feel as if I'm going on a little vacation. I can relax, put my feet up and become transported to a new world...a world that has, naturally, a perfect hero just waiting to whisk me away! These are stories to remember, containing moments to treasure.

Silhouette Desire novels are romantic love stories—sensuous yet emotional. As a reader, you not only see the hero and heroine fall in love, you also feel what they're feeling.

In upcoming books look for some of your favorite Silhouette Desire authors: Joan Hohl, BJ James, Linda Lael Miller and Diana Palmer.

So enjoy!

Lucia Macro
Senior Editor

CAIT
LONDON
ANGEL VS. MACLEAN

SILHOUETTE *Desire*

Published by Silhouette Books New York

America's Publisher of Contemporary Romance

SILHOUETTE BOOKS
300 East 42nd St., New York, N.Y. 10017

Copyright © 1990 by Lois Kleinsasser-Testerman

All rights reserved. Except for use in any review,
the reproduction or utilization of this work in
whole or in part in any form by any electronic,
mechanical or other means, now known or
hereafter invented, including xerography,
photocopying and recording, or in any information
storage or retrieval system, is forbidden without
the permission of Silhouette Books, 300 E. 42nd St.,
New York, N.Y. 10017

ISBN: 0-373-05593-5

First Silhouette Books printing September 1990

All the characters in this book are fictitious. Any
resemblance to actual persons, living or dead, is
purely coincidental.

®: Trademark used under license and
registered in the United States Patent and
Trademark Office and in other countries.

Printed in the U.S.A.

Books by Cait London

Silhouette Desire

The Loving Season #502
Angel vs. MacLean #593

CAIT LONDON

lives in the Missouri Ozarks but grew up in Washington and still loves craggy mountains and the Pacific coast. She's a full-time secretary, a history buff and an avid reader who knows her way around computers. She grew up painting—landscapes and wildlife—but is now committed to writing and enjoying her three creative daughters. Cait has big plans for her future—learning to fish, taking short trips for research and meeting people. She also writes as Cait Logan and has won *Romantic Times*'s Best New Romance Writer award for 1986.

For Lana, the last little bird

One

J. D. MacLean hated waiting, especially in the early morning. He scowled at the row of clocks on the Denver airport wall, reading the assorted world times impatiently. Normally he'd be seated at his desk, methodically sorting his work while his secretary recited the day's appointments. Carefully folding his stock market report and tucking it beneath his arm, he rose from the hard, molded plastic seat.

Dressed in a tight red dress, a passing woman smiled slowly at him. At forty-four, J.D. recognized the invitation and acknowledged it with a curt nod, then walked to view the jets that were coming and going. The May wind swept across the concrete, thrusting so hard against the workers that they had to lean into it to keep their balance, their uniforms flapping against their bodies.

Beyond the window, a big passenger jet cruised down its designated path to position for takeoff. Soon another jet would bring his grandson, Travis MacLean Malone, re-

turning from a week-long stay with his paternal grandmother.

J.D. knew how much Travis needed him. The five-year-
old was an orphan, and J.D., as his sole guardian, had
promised that his grandson would be the first priority in his
life.

In one sweep a December avalanche had carried away the
lives of his daughter and son-in-law. Remembering his son-
in-law's smashed car, J.D. could feel the pain rip through
him again.

Daisy. As if it were yesterday, J.D. could hear his daughter's bright, "Hi, Daddy! Guess what happened at school
today?" He could see the look on her face when she carefully spread her crayon drawing of a truck on his lap.

I love you, Daddy. How many times had Daisy's drowsy,
childish whisper echoed through his sleepless nights?
Blinking against the unexpected dampness behind his eyelids, J.D. fought the wave of sheer loneliness that was
washing over him.

Then there were Travis's questions. *When is Mommy and
Daddy coming home, Grandpa? Is heaven a nice place?*

J.D.'s grazed knuckles stung as they brushed against his
slacks. Swinging his fist into a wall at dawn was a stupid
thing to do; death and fate were hard opponents to fight.

He'd just never had enough time for Daisy. Twenty-one
years ago his wife had tossed a stack of bills into his face.
When she walked out the door, leaving him with the infant
Daisy, he'd really tried. But between starting his trucking
business and picking up odd singing spots in taverns, there
had just never been enough time—

J.D. ran the fingertips of his other hand across the dam-
aged knuckles. Raising a child would be different this time.
Daisy had left him a precious part of herself, and Travis
needed him desperately. Idly watching the travelers flow
through the spacious airport, J.D. allowed the warmth he
felt for his grandson to curl about him. Though he was still

too quiet and insecure since his parents' accident, Travis was a MacLean down to his small cowboy boots.

This summer and thereafter, J.D. promised silently, Travis would have what every five-year-old boy needed—sunshine, laughter and love enough to fill him.

In the week prior to Travis's visit, J.D. had worked day and night to swing the final stages of his business move to Denver. Now, with MacLean Investments securely lodged there, he could begin working out details for spending time in the mountains with Travis.

J.D. mentally checked off the various concerns that he had brought under the umbrella of his business. Encompassing a cross-country trucking line with fast delivery service, MacLean Investments also provided tourist travel. Through the years he'd also snared a neat amount of related investments in the stock market. The intricate composite was the fruit of a life of sweat, blood and sleepless nights. Now Travis needed him more. By working overtime with the help of his well-oiled organization, using a hot line and a commuter airplane, J.D. intended to create a schedule that would allow him more time for his grandson.

J.D. smiled slowly, thinking of Travis's bedroom in the Denver penthouse. Adorned with a new bicycle, a fishing rod and an assortment of other necessities, the room reflected the way J.D. intended to spend the summer—playing with his grandson.

J.D. pictured the majestic view of the Rockies from the floor-to-ceiling windows in Travis's bedroom. J.D. had grown up in the mountains and he wanted Travis to enjoy the same wild, beautiful scenery. With patience and love, his black-haired grandson would soon reflect his MacLean heritage. Before the accident Travis had been a regular terror, but then the MacLeans were not known for breeding gentle stock. J.D. thought briefly of his rough-and-tumble brothers, Mac and Rafe, who lived in the San Juan mountains in Southern Colorado. Though Mac had recently married, Rafe was still in pursuit of his "true ladylove."

A honey-colored blonde swept through the busy waiting area as though she owned it, and J.D. felt the muscles of his jaw tighten. Dressed in a custom-tailored business suit that clung to her tall frame, the blonde's back was to him. Gliding on marvelously long, tanned legs, she came to a stop before the overhead screens displaying the airline schedules.

She ran a manicured hand through her multilayered, shoulder-length mane of hair. Gripping a worn briefcase, she shifted restlessly on her practical black pumps.

A shaft of anger and hatred shot through J.D., catching him by surprise. Hell, he thought, irritated with himself, when a man had been gut-punched as many times as he had, he should be able to control his reactions better.

But somehow *she* lurked in every beautiful face. A slant of a brow, a curve of soft cheek beneath rich blonde hair still beckoned to him. Even in memory, Katherine Dalton Kelly knew how to land her punches.

Kat. He'd almost killed himself denying the love she'd offered, and in return she'd cut him to emotional ribbons. J.D.'s stomach contracted painfully with memories that went back twenty years.

Three giggling teenage girls passed him on the airport concourse. He caught the flirtatious looks that drifted down his navy-blue business suit to his expensive Western boots. J.D. nodded absently at them. When he'd first met Kat she'd been that age, the sweetly innocent baby-sitter to his daughter, Daisy, after his wife's abrupt decision.

He shook his head to clear it of memories of the painful events of the years that had followed their first meeting. The need to pay Katherine back, to knock her off her high horse, had gnawed at him for years, and now he was headquartered in Denver, the time just might have come. He knew that when Katherine found out about his partnership with her sister Irish, there'd be hell to pay. Yes, he was definitely anticipating a meeting with the haughty Ms. Kelly. But getting Travis settled had to come first.

J.D. again allowed his gaze to stroll over the blonde's elegant backside as she studied the overhead monitors. The gray suit did nothing to hide her trim, leggy figure and the delicate curve of her hips. He shifted on his dress boots, restless as his body suddenly tensed.

Still impatient, he slashed a look around the waiting area. He hadn't meant to get trapped in old frustrations, snared by a mass of honey-blonde hair.

He rubbed a hand across the back of his taut neck, angry at himself for not having better control after all these years. Travis didn't need any more problems than he already had—

The blonde turned slightly, her smoky-gray eyes scanning the area, and J.D. stopped breathing. A jolt of white-hot anger shot through him as he recognized the unmistakeable face of Katherine Kelly.

Denver's Avenging Angel, as the news media termed her, was a tough, brilliant attorney, dedicated to her causes and career. J.D. pressed his lips together firmly. But angels were supposed to have selfless, caring hearts, and J.D. knew all too well that Katherine's could be bought. Anything she did, she did for profit.

Pushing away from the wall, he found himself walking toward her as anger took over. With Katherine, a man had to take his shots where he could, when he could.

And she owed him a lot of punches.

As though sensing him she turned slowly, lifting her gaze to his face. "Hello, Kat," J.D. said easily, despite the rage that was churning inside him.

"J.D." She was cool—he had to give her credit for that. Only a brief widening of her eyes and a slight loss of color from her cheeks betrayed her surprise at seeing him. She nodded and turned back to resume her study of the arrivals listed on the monitor. When he didn't move on, she glanced at him again and asked coolly, "Don't you need to be somewhere else? Anywhere else?"

"We'll probably be meeting often. Denver is my new home," he answered, watching her expression.

"So I heard." She tossed the sunlit mane of hair back carelessly. The legendary Kelly diamond glittered on her left hand, and J.D. felt the length of his tall body contract. She still wore it, though she'd been widowed five years. She'd probably been cautioned by the insurance company about the risk of thefts, but Katherine never gave an inch.

The diamond wouldn't be a copy, either, he was sure. Synthetics weren't listed in Kat's manual of style.

"I'd have thought Denver's avenging angel would have time for an old friend." He paused for effect, then added, "Angel—that label really draws donations from the bleeding hearts, doesn't it?"

Turning fully toward him, she met his eyes uncompromisingly. "I have a busy day, J.D. I'm not in the mood for chitchat."

But J.D. couldn't resist probing the controlled emotions beneath her expressionless face. Championing underdogs, she'd faced many courtrooms, presenting brilliant cases with that sharp mind she had. When she'd properly set the stage, she would pull out her explosive fire to scoop the jurists into her corner.

Katherine wouldn't be so controlled when she discovered his partnership with Irish, J.D. wagered. But he could wait, choosing the time and place on his terms. Reaching out to slide a finger down her cheek, J.D. found himself enjoying the way Katherine lifted her chin and moved slightly.

"Go away, J.D.," she said levelly. "Before I call the airport police."

He chuckled, admiring the low, almost steamy quality of her voice even in anger. Using Irish as bait, he planned to deepen that anger. All the same, as he traced the lift of her brow and the sweep of the lashes that shadowed her cheeks, J.D. felt another jarring punch to his midsection. Katherine might prefer to keep their duel removed from intimacy, but he had no such restrictions. In fact, he intended to pursue it to the limit. "You haven't changed in years, Kat," he said softly.

Her head jerked back as though she'd taken a blow, and within their slightly slanted shape, her pupils flashed his image back at him. J.D. liked seeing her eyes change. The irises turned a smoky, passionate gray, though her face remained untouched by emotion. Her eyes reminded him of a mountain pool reflecting a thunderous sky—with gold aspen leaves skimming the water's surface and catching glimpses of the sun.

His throat tightened, the way it did whenever he thought of her marriage to Big Jim Kelly. "So, *Angel*," he said, dipping the name into a cynical tone. "How are the Kelly millions?"

For a moment she went pale, but the only movement on her face was a slight tightening of her full lips. "Keep baiting me, J.D., and someday the sport might kill you."

J.D. raised his hand again and watched her almost—but not quite—flinch as he rubbed his knuckles down her jawline. She seemed to vibrate beneath his touch, and the thought gave him a measure of satisfaction. He'd waited years to strike beneath the veneer. "I always liked a good fight, Kat."

"I'd rip you apart." She breathed shakily, lifting her head back slightly as though she regretted giving him even an inch. The gold flecks in her eyes caught the light, shimmering with anger.

"Really?" he drawled, smiling slightly. "My knees are shaking now."

The long, elegantly trimmed nails sank into her briefcase. "They should be."

The pulse at the base of her neck beat against the expensive, creamy material of her blouse and he allowed his gaze to move lower. Beneath the long strand of perfectly matched pearls it was all there—the slender softness, the woman she chose to hide beneath the fashionable suit. He could almost feel her breathe, feel her fighting for control.

Katherine flicked back a long strand of hair from her temple, revealing a tiny pearl stud in her earlobe. She wore a minimum of cosmetics and her beauty was classic. She was like that, J.D. decided, her understated elegance written in the new, silvery shades of her hair. Cool, remote and just as beautiful as when she'd turned her back on him to marry the owner of the Kelly millions.

He saw her fingers—slender, pale and without polish— flutter restlessly against the briefcase.

It was a nervous gesture. He knew he was getting to her then, and a wave of sheer pleasure washed over him. When she was nervous, Katherine moved her hands much as another woman might smooth her hair. But Katherine wasn't "another woman." She was the one who had haunted him for years....

"Don't try to get to me, J.D.," she warned lightly, flicking back her sleeve to check her practical wristwatch. "I do detest come-ons in airports. They're so cheap, and I'm really not a game player."

He forced a smile, angry with himself for letting her score a hit with the reference to his struggling years. She'd caught him unprepared and landed an unexpected punch, taking him back to the hard times he'd rather forget.

He glanced up as they announced the arrival of Travis's flight. Trimming Katherine's claws would have to wait for another time. He gave her one last, evaluating look. "See you around . . . Angel."

As J.D. walked toward one of the gates, Katherine forced herself to stand quietly and study the arrivals monitor once more.

She wasn't in the mood to meet Maxy, an old friend skimming across the country to her family; in fact Katherine really wasn't in the mood for anything but hours—no, months—of rest. She forced her fingers to ease their tight grip on her briefcase. She was too brittle to cross swords with J. D. MacLean, even verbally, and the effort to remain cool throughout their meeting had cost her.

J.D. The initials were like a curse.

She had heard that he'd recently transferred his business to Denver; she should have been more prepared for an unexpected encounter.

Closing her eyes, she willed herself to think of a cool, rippling, forest stream. It was a trick she'd learned to use in her harried courtroom life, and the mental minivacation usually restored her self-control.

But this time when she closed her eyes, she saw only J.D...the eyes so dark that the pupils were not defined, the sharp angles of his face, hard and unrelenting.

Dark-skinned, with equal parts of Scottish, Spanish and Ute Indian mixed in his veins, J.D. was all savage beneath his Wall Street trappings, Kat thought. Straight black lashes, probably a reminder of his Ute heritage, were his only softening features.

His thick, neatly cropped hair brushed the collar of his suit. Just enough silver in his hair gave him the air of a reputable businessman.

He looked tough; he *was* tough, she corrected herself. But J.D. exuded a primitive, careless aura that attracted women like hummingbirds to honeysuckle. As an entrepreneur he was a financial wizard, scooping up small businesses and folding them into his personal empire.

Her fingers still trembled. She should have been better prepared. He'd purposely stepped on her torn nerves, she decided. And she had barely contained her immediate and savage response to him. She'd wanted to rip into him tooth and claw.

As a professional, hard-working lawyer, she'd worked for years to be able to face men—any man—on an equal level. When she and J.D. met again—and they would—she didn't intend to let him nettle her. He'd jumped into her home arena and he'd have to take the consequences.

Next time she'd be ready.

Taking a deep, steadying breath, she pressed her lips together. As a man he was in her past. He could bat his outrageously long lashes elsewhere. Katherine liked her life simple, filled with nasty criminals and tough judges, and she didn't intend to let J.D. complicate things. Even if they had to share Denver.

She was just tired, she rationalized. Otherwise J.D. wouldn't have been able to bring the anger ripping out of her after all these years.

Maybe Irish was right; maybe she did just need a good rest.

She'd fought too many battles, yet there was always just one more cause that needed her—one more.... In her last case, supporting a rape victim, Katherine had almost lost her self-control. It had been a big case, one that had had her ulcer acting up.

When she won the case Katherine had been near collapse. Rubbing her aching temples now, Katherine remembered how edgy she'd been, the way she'd almost cost her clients. Her high level of performance demanded breaks from work and enough sleep. Running from office to court and back again, she was too wound up. Somewhere in the maze she'd lost that keen edge of control, lashing out at a judge and almost destroying her poise with a gush of tears in the courtroom.

The moment had been devastating, a personal black mark that was her own deep shame. *She hated being weak.*

In her profession, loss of control could easily cost a life. She'd always kept a distance between her emotions and her clients, but now she feared that the clear logic that was her trademark was getting sloppy. After devoting herself to her career for so long, Katherine could easily see it slipping down the proverbial drain.

She had to get her life back in hand. She'd been running too fast, working too hard, and it had all caught up with her. She needed to balance the rest of her life, explore her needs.

She ran her thumb along the broad wedding band on her left hand, tracing its outline. Once Big Jim had listened and helped and supported. She missed that companionship.

A young couple paused to share a lingering kiss, and Katherine frowned. Toying now with her lapel pin, she drifted back in thought to another time. J.D. had kissed her like that—as though she were the most precious thing in his life. Each caress had lingered, made her hunger for more. She would have given him her soul on a platter.

Giving him her body had been an experience she'd never forgotten.

Katherine closed her eyes, still hating him. Twenty years ago she hadn't had a chance. J.D. had affected her like that—taking charge, making decisions for her. Katherine had been just out of high school, looking for a summer job before college. When J.D.'s wife had walked out on him, Katherine had stepped in as baby-sitter to the struggling trucker's six-month-old daughter.

She'd loved him with all her young heart. Briefly she'd felt her love returned. Then J.D. had stepped on her and made the decision that she was too young.

She had been crushed and furious. J.D. had handed down his dictum without the slightest thought that she might stand by him. That she really might love him.

Katherine had walked away from him, unable then to return the hurt he'd dealt her.

After J.D.'s monumental decision, Big Jim had soothed her like a sweet ocean breeze. She'd taken his advice, his scholarship and then his ring. Always there for her, Big Jim had been more of a friend than a lover. She'd appreciated the way he didn't pry into her emotions. Her husband had offered support when she needed it and had kept his distance from her career.

Visiting J.D. six years later, she had had the pleasure of seeing his expression shift from disbelief to rage. Maybe she had been wrong to let him think she'd married Big Jim for his money; but then she'd needed the revenge of seeing J.D.'s pain and disbelief.

Katherine rubbed her arm briskly. She still missed Big Jim's anchor in her life. Since his death she'd focused everything on her career, working feverishly for causes that had left her exhausted. No wonder J.D. had been able to catch her broadside today.

Her gaze followed a white jet stream across the brilliant blue sky. Maxy's plane would be unloading within minutes, and Katherine badly needed her friend's bubbly company. The two-hour stopover before Maxy continued to Seattle would allow them time to catch up on Maxy's four children and share a laugh over cocktails.

Katherine smiled briefly. Maxy was just the type of emotional Band-Aid she needed right now to soothe the unexpected bruise left by J.D. Later on, she'd give more thought to Irish's suggestion that she spend some time relaxing at her sister's bed-and-breakfast inn.

Katherine felt her smile widen at the thought of Irish's loving care and her beloved but ramshackle turn-of-the-century house.

"Hi, Grandpa!" Travis escaped from the stewardess who had been holding his hand through the entrance gate and ran toward J.D.

Scooping up the little boy, J.D. noted how tightly Travis's arms locked around his neck. The boy's small body was trembling.

"Hey, scout," J.D. murmured gently against Travis's black hair. "I'm glad you're home."

Travis continued to hold him tightly, and J.D. moved out of the other passengers' way. Against his neck Travis muttered, "I won't go back. I won't. I'm not ever leaving you again. What if something happens to you?"

Then he squirmed to the floor and stood looking up at J.D. "I'm ready to go home now," he said solemnly.

Later that night, standing over Travis's bed, J.D. eased the boy's thumb from his mouth and frowned, recognizing that the habit had returned. His grandson had a lot of healing to do. They both did.

Two

Mandy, Katherine's secretary, tossed a thick file onto a leaning stack of papers on Katherine's desk. "You were here late again last night," Mandy accused, looking over the rims of her small, narrow glasses.

"Mmm." Already her trip to the airport yesterday seemed days ago. Katherine snatched at the new file and ripped it open. "Is this the Krevis versus Neman file? Ah...," Her finger traced its way down to one line and tapped it carefully. "Here he says he didn't know the building was about to be condemned. But Commissioner Rebloski said..."

She jerked another file from the bottom of the stack and opened it, again using her finger to find what she was looking for. "That's it. Of course Krevis knew the building was going to be condemned. Rebloski's secretary told him it was on the list. We've got him, Mandy."

"Uh-huh," Mandy answered flatly, crossing her arms. "Did you manage to squeeze in a few hours of shut-eye?"

When Katherine jotted down notes from the two files without answering, Mandy shook her head. "A Kelly board member is waiting in the outer office," she said with a sigh. "He wants to know if you'll see him about some proposed merger. And the newspaper reporter is on line two. He wants to know if you're ready to disclose anything about that rip-off salesman going door to door, selling health insurance to the elderly. He wants to warn the public—"

"That's a good idea." Katherine picked up the telephone and began talking while Mandy scribbled her a note: Irish is on line one. I'll tell her you'll call her back when you're free.

Katherine nodded and continued her conversation with the newspaperman, pressing the flat of her hand against her stomach, where her ulcer was burning. Mandy stared at her for a hard moment, then handed her a bottle of antacid tablets. She took away Katherine's full cup of coffee, replacing it with iced mineral water.

Three hours later, Katherine found Mandy's note and picked up the phone to dial her sister.

Irish was as whimsical and gay as her name, a woman born to comfort others. She had a personality like sunshine and flowers and sweet, Colorado mountain air. Katherine not only loved her sister, she liked her.

Katherine leaned back in her chair, warming to Irish's concerned voice. "You're always doing it, you know," Irish said. "Overworking, never taking time to relax. How many times have I asked you to take it easy? How many times have I invited you to the inn? You need to rest, Kat," she finished sternly. "What would Mother and Dad say if they knew you were within hours of Kodiak and didn't manage to come let me take care of you?"

"I've got too much work piled up now, Irish. Think what would happen to my practice if I took off whenever I wanted to. Let's talk about your business," Katherine threw in quickly before Irish could catch her second wind.

Katherine noted the distinct pause at the other end of the line. "Business?" Irish asked softly in a tone that caught Katherine's undivided attention. It had that silky, who, me? quality that Irish's voice took on when she got caught red-handed.

"Yes, business. Your bed-and-breakfast. How's the money pit holding up? Any new sunken floors or leaky roofs?"

"Ah . . . business is fine," Irish answered in a distracted tone. "I'm just worried about you. Are you eating all right, Kat? You eat all that junk food when you're in a hurry, and I really think—"

"Getting a lot of reservations?" Katherine asked, not willing to be thrown off the track.

"Lots. You're getting plenty of rest, aren't you?"

"Plenty. Are you still operating in the red? Are you sure you don't want me to help?"

"Hell's bells, no. I didn't call you for help, Kat. I'm just worried about you."

"Did you get the rewiring done?" Katherine asked, continuing to push.

"Of course I did. It was dangerous—"

"How much did you pay for the job? Did you have to go to the bank again?"

"Kat," Irish said hotly. "I'm your sister, not a hostile witness. Anyway, my partner takes care of—"

"Partner?" There it was, Katherine decided. She'd offered many times to help Irish, and her sister had steadfastly refused. Now Irish felt guilty.

"Ah . . . J. D. MacLean." Irish dropped the name as carefully as a French lace handkerchief. "Katherine, stop playing attorney. I'm calling to see if you're—"

"J. D. MacLean," Katherine repeated dully, the image of his tough face swimming before her. "He's a shark," she stated distinctly. "Have you signed papers with him, Irish?"

Her sister hesitated, then answered firmly, "Yes, I did. We're partners. He's loaning me enough money to get out of debt, and he's managing the books."

Katherine felt like a quicksand victim being sucked under the mire. J.D. had her baby sister in hock! "If you needed help, why didn't you call me?" she demanded.

"Please don't be hurt, Kat. It's a business arrangement. You know I like to do things myself. You . . . well, you just sort of . . . take over," Irish explained hesitantly. "Kat, please try to understand. With J.D. it's different—that's all."

"I'll bet," Katherine said slowly, quietly.

Irish began again. "There you go, assuming the worst. This partnership is going to work out. Dealing with criminals and all, you just have a suspicious mind. J.D. is true-blue."

"I can think of more accurate adjectives," Katherine muttered. She frowned, crumpling a piece of paper with restless fingers as she thought of J.D.'s dark, confident face yesterday. He'd known then that she would object to the partnership. No doubt he was in his lair, just waiting for her to call. Well, she wouldn't disappoint him. Mr. MacLean needed to know he couldn't go collecting her kid sister.

"Coming to see me then, Kat?" Irish asked hopefully. "I'll tell you all about it, if you do. Oh, it's so exciting. . . ."

"I have another call. I'll call you back." When Katherine replaced the receiver on its cradle, her fingers were aching with the tension. "J. D. MacLean," she repeated dully. "It would be just like him to take advantage of Irish."

She spread her hands over the papers scattered across her desk. Closing her eyes, she allowed them to rest for the first time since sunrise. If she was going to talk with J.D., she needed every drop of inner strength. A week's lack of sleep scraped at her weary nerves, and she rubbed her temples, searching for a calm that would not come.

Leaning back in her mauve office chair, Katherine looked out the window of her legal suite to view Denver.

The blue sky, tall buildings and mountain backdrop didn't present an answer. She was on edge and tired, but she had to take J.D. out of Irish's personal and financial picture. Her baby sister wasn't up for grabs.

In her experience, Katherine had seen many bitter enemies position themselves for a final showdown. Her gut feeling now was that she needed to rip J.D. apart once and forever.

There had to be a loophole. Perhaps if she talked to J.D. and actually scanned the partnership agreement she would find something.

Her modern, brass and tinted-glass suite often soothed her nerves, but not now. She rose, walking across the thick, off-white carpeting in her stocking feet. Flexing her toes into the shaggy nap, Katherine let her gaze skim over the volumes of legal cases lining her bookshelves and wandered to the windows.

The new MacLean Building towered over smaller structures in downtown Denver. Cut from dark granite with mirrorlike windows, the building resembled its owner—harsh, unyielding and impregnable. At the very top, Katherine knew, J.D. stalked in his lair—knowing she'd call him about Irish.

Katherine touched the conference button on her telephone. In seconds her call had passed through four secretaries to the inner sanctum of J. D. MacLean. "MacLean here."

"Preying upon any defenseless women at the moment, J.D.?" she asked lightly, letting her gaze drift to Irish's picture on her desk. Katherine rubbed her temple. It was maddening that Irish had turned to J.D., unaware of the possible dangers.

There was a pause on the other end of the line, just long enough for her to visualize his slow, predatory grin. "Irish, you mean?" he said then. "I've been expecting your call, Kat."

J.D.'s raspy, deep voice invaded Katherine's contemporary office. His tone held just enough masculine arrogance to jangle her already uneasy nerves. She wanted to see his face, explore his expression. Just what did he feel? What would it take to soothe him or to set him off?

"Irish should have called me when she got into financial trouble, J.D."

"You'd take over," he said quietly.

So he was still throwing punches, was he? She could feel anger ripple through her like a hot, electric wire. "I'll start a war you'll never forget, you backwoods vulture," she began huskily as the anger grew. "Just how much will it take to call you off?"

"I haven't got time to discuss the matter now. I'm in the middle of a meeting," J.D. cut in. "I'm tied up until ten tonight. Show up here then."

The line went dead, and Katherine's anger shimmered and changed, threatening to devour her. J.D. was like that: setting up shots to his best advantage.

She crumpled a note tightly in her hand, then flung it aside. "Show up here then," she repeated between her teeth. "You just bet I will."

J.D. stood at the windows, looking across the blanket of lights that twinkled in the city night. He glanced at the flat gold watch on his wrist. At a quarter of ten Travis would be safely entrenched in his bed, sleeping deeply among his trucks and stuffed animals. He'd be dreaming about leaving for the mountains in two days. Filled with questions, Travis had kept his sitter busy until he curled up with his favorite blanket after a long, reassuring telephone talk with J.D.

Travis needed attention, and J.D. had taken his grandson's calls throughout the day, even when it meant making his staff and board members wait. The afternoon priority had been pet shopping with the boy, with the end results a scruffy, mongrel puppy appropriately named Puddles and a wide grin from J.D.'s grandson.

Looking down at the MacLean Building's parking lot, he saw a white Jeep gliding to a stop. A moment later Katherine stepped beneath the streetlights. Dressed in loose slacks and a jacket, she moved across the lot to the night watchman's entrance.

She'd haunted him for years, and now here she was, moving towards him with that smooth dancer's stride, all pride and anger, her head held high. He remembered her hair at the airport, blended shades of silvery gold and brown; the colors intrigued him.

Rubbing the Ute talisman beneath his shirt had become a habit when J.D. was deep in thought. Performing the gesture almost automatically, he thought about Katherine.

After all these years it was quite a feeling to know that Kat wanted to sink her claws into him. Now with Irish as bait, he'd torment the hell out of Katherine for the sheer pleasure of it.

He remembered her nervousness, those restless, slim fingers with the blazing Kelly diamond. A primitive urge rose in him suddenly, tightening the cords in his jaw. *He wanted that damned brand off Katherine's hand.*

His thoughts skipped back twenty years. He rubbed an old scar that crossed his temple and slashed one eyebrow. It ached at times, like memories of Katherine. Katherine had had a way about her then—all fresh, mountain flowers— and something deeper.

Looking back, J.D. recognized how Katherine had pushed herself into his life, convincing him she should babysit Daisy. There was steel in Kat even back then, she'd been the do-gooder type—the cause fighter with endless legs, who had pinpointed a struggling trucker with a baby to support.

And covering the steel was the silky-soft skin.

His mouth was suddenly dry, needing the bite of a good, strong drink. Memories of Katherine—his Kat—did that to him.

She'd wanted him then, he'd sensed it in every soft curve of her body, in every sweet, hesitant smile. He had held himself back, aching for her lithe, young body. She had dressed in T-shirts and worn jeans that fitted her long legs tightly. She was all smoky-gray eyes and silky hair that swayed, brushing her hips as she walked.

How noble he'd been, fighting the haunting attraction—a virgin, Katherine couldn't have known how she'd caused him to ache.

Finally, one night he'd fallen completely beneath her spell and allowed himself to forget reality. Katherine had tipped her face up to his and given that low, sultry laugh—as though life were a mystery and she held the key.

Taking her and remembering her sweet sigh of surprise and kissing away her tears were things J.D. had found haunting him forever thereafter. Just moments—or was it a century later?—with Katherine curled sweetly in his arms, reality had come ripping into him. She was too young. He couldn't saddle her with the burdens of his bills and his daughter. She deserved a life of her own ahead, not long hours spent trying to build a business.

Okay, he'd handled the moment badly. Too roughly, because the gut-wrenching emotions were ripping him apart. He'd made the break as clean as he could, knowing that she'd fight him.

He closed his eyes, recalling the shock in her wide eyes, the trembling of her lips as his words knifed into her... *You're too damn young. Now get the hell out of here.*

By God, she'd coolly cut him in half. Turned on him and used her claws to lash him to ribbons. *How did it feel, knowing you dangled me at the end of your string, controlling me—making me fall in love with...?* She had hesitated, fighting tears, then continued. *Well, you're done now, J.D. Anytime I want you making decisions for me, I'll ask. You're not a phase with me anymore, J.D.—I hate you! You think you're the almighty, handing down judgments from on high. I'm not a child. I make my own decisions. You come near me again and I'll shoot you.*

Within two weeks, young Katherine had been in college and headed for a law degree. A friend of her family, Big Jim Kelly, soon had her tucked under his wing. Katherine worked with his extensive legal department while she was in college, the forty-year-old millionaire squiring her around Denver.

Visiting her family, she'd flaunted her relationship with Big Jim before J.D. Older than J.D., Big Jim could give Katherine everything, while J.D. was still struggling with bills and a baby.

Six years after their lovemaking, Katherine had dropped by J.D.'s office, displaying her wedding ring. She'd been out for blood; he'd read it in her stormy-gray eyes and the sharp angle of her chin. J.D. had been drinking too much then, but her words had still branded him like a hot sword as the story came out. *Big Jim wouldn't have me as a virgin, J.D. He was the one I really wanted. So you see, you served your purpose after all....*

His brutal kiss then, a punishment for his sweet Kat, had brought blood to her lips. "Can Big Jim match that, Kat?" he'd asked afterward. He was drunk and out of bounds, he knew, but with all the pain in him, he'd had to lash out.

Katherine had returned the blow in spades.

She'd wiped her hand across her mouth as though removing his taste. "He's better, J.D. Much better," she'd replied, smiling coldly. "And he gives me what I want." Then she had turned, smoothed her hair and walked out to her expensive convertible.

J.D. frowned, still stroking the dark green stone tied to his throat by a leather thong. *Katherine was finally moving toward him—the time had come to play out the game.* After all these years he had something Katherine wanted badly. "The tigress protecting her cub," he murmured as he dimmed the lights and started the low, romantic music.

Katherine couldn't possibly know that J.D. thought of Irish as his friend, a special one with a talent that healed. For now it suited him to bait Kat, and he would. By God, he swore, he'd pay her back for every bottle of scotch he'd downed to forget her. Katherine Dalton Kelly would be picking up the tab for every sleepless, aching night he'd had thinking of her. "Angel, you are going to squirm," he promised darkly.

Katherine would fight tooth and nail for her friends and family. J.D. reluctantly admitted he admired that quality, the steely strength that had once locked him out of her heart.

When the buzzer sounded in a muted tone, he bit back his roiling emotions and opened the door to her.

Katherine entered his suite in a swirl of creamy fabrics. Her gaze took in his light blue dress shirt, sleeves folded back at the wrist, paused, then ran the length of his navy slacks to his stocking feet. Her haughty look suggested she'd estimated the cost of his tailor and found it lacking. "J.D."

"Kat," he returned evenly, admiring the way the fabric clung to the length of her legs. When she turned, he noted the soft curve of her breast beneath the satin vest. "Would you like a drink?"

She sighed, looking around the walnut walls with the large, slashing paintings. She prowled, moving across the burnt-sienna carpeting to the massive, paper-covered desk, then to the angular, contemporary sectional couch. She studied the plaque citing his Good-Buddy award from a convict rehabilitation center. "I don't drink," she answered finally. "I'd rather talk about Irish."

"Indulge me," he challenged and watched her eyes widen fractionally. He was going to enjoy seeing those gray eyes smolder with anger. This time it was his game.

Her long neck went back, the dim light catching on her hair as she turned to face him. He resisted the urge to reach out and take a handful of the tumbling mass. "We're hav-

ing dinner," he said calmly. "The chef is waiting for my call.
Is there something special you'd like to order?"

Her gray eyes seemed to spit at him as he threw the first
punch, laying out the ground rules on his terms. She shook
her head. "It's been a long day. I'd prefer to come right to
the point."

"Over dinner then," he drawled slowly, guessing that her
anger was rising. Holding her gaze, he walked to his well-
stocked bar to pour himself a glass of iced mineral water. He
squeezed a slice of lime into the liquid and tossed in the rind.
"I suggest you relax," he offered bluntly. "I haven't had a
perfect day myself."

The rounded line of her jaw hardened and her fingers
tightened on the small purse she wore at her waist. "Suit
yourself."

"Oh, I intend to." J.D. pushed an intercom buzzer.
"Henri, I'm ready. The usual and—" he flicked a glance at
Katherine, who had begun walking restlessly around the
room again. "—lobster and your special guest salad. I'll call
within fifteen minutes after service or you can go on home.
Thanks."

Katherine's beauty hadn't changed, he decided later,
watching her pick at her lobster. Enhanced by the candlelight, her slanting eyes seemed to glow as they assessed him
warily. He liked that—Katherine looking at him, appraising him while her restless hands toyed with the silver platters and dinnerware. She was obviously waiting now,
reminding herself that the dinner was only a minor battle,
not the war.

They ate in silence, but the soft music did not soothe his
nerves, either. She pushed her food with her fork, flicking
him impatient glances. He noted the dark circles beneath her
eyes, the pale transparency of her skin in the candlelight. So
she was tired, was she? He'd put in a few hard times himself.

"Finished?" he asked, rising from the table. Katherine nodded curtly and began to rise, too. J.D. bent quickly, placing a hand on the back of the chair.

Their eyes clashed as he slowly pulled it out from her, setting the pace of her move toward freedom. "Allow me."

She threw him a look that told him where to go, and he felt a warm blush of satisfaction. There was something about taunting her that gave him deep, immense pleasure.

Katherine walked to the ceiling-high windows, rubbing her palms together, her back to him.

J.D. caught himself watching her neat backside with a less than casual interest. The thought that she could still jerk him around was an irritation he forced aside. Settling onto the couch, he held his iced mineral water on his stomach and looked up at her. "Well? You can sit down, Kat. Or are you too frightened of me?"

She compressed her lips with anger, but eased herself into a chair opposite him. As she crossed her legs with a soft swish, J.D. felt a surge of sheer desire. The satin vest rose and fell and she sighed quietly, looking into the starlit night as if she wished she were anywhere else.

With anyone else. The thought unaccountably nettled J.D.

Slowly she scraped the rough, beige upholstery with her long nails, repeating the pattern. J.D. shifted his back against the couch, almost feeling the nails on his flesh. *Damn!*

Katherine could keep the world at bay, but not him. Not any longer, J.D. decided. Her love for Irish was almost her only weakness, and he intended to use his leverage to the best advantage.

"Just what would it take to buy you off, J.D.? Irish hasn't a ghost of an idea what she owes you." Katherine's voice was smooth, but husky with tension.

He could almost feel the tightness in that long, slender throat, and the thought warmed him. He watched the ice cubes float in the liquid in his glass. "Even you couldn't write a check for what I want, Kat."

Katherine's eyes opened wide, allowing him to see the silvery, flashing depths. "You can't have her, J.D. I won't allow it. You'll have to put some other poor woman through a strainer."

J.D. leveled his next shot. "I like Irish. I wouldn't play rough on this one, if I were you, Kat. Irish doesn't know the game. You could lose her. You'll have to deal with me."

For a moment the restless fingers quieted and slowly flexed. "I think we can settle the matter without her."

"You mean the Kelly millions will bail Irish out? She's a soft-hearted woman, but your little sister has more backbone than you know. Maybe she's tired of you managing her life."

"I can handle Irish's money problems, J.D. My personal business manager will call for the figures."

"Your money can go to hell," J.D. stated quietly, watching her eyes. "I won't talk to him. Irish and I have a deal."

"Don't stand in my way. Come close to my sister, and I'll—"

"I am standing in your way," J.D. said simply. "You just have to be in control, don't you? Everything is black and white with you—the good guys and the bad guys. Would you believe that I helped her out because I like her, Kat?"

"Not a chance. You're geared for takeovers."

He smiled at that. He had the right bait. And he intended to take part of Katherine's sweet hide for his revenge. "Maybe I am. Maybe you and the whole Kelly empire couldn't stop me—if I really wanted Irish. Or any woman."

Her eyes glowed and flashed at him. "Damn you, J.D. Don't toy with me. I'm not interested in your affairs with other women. Just leave Irish alone. I'll pay her bills with ungodly interest."

"Oh, you'll pay, Angel," he murmured, watching her taut face. Her hair shimmered in the dim light. In the shadows her slanting eyes were luminous depths.

Katherine's flawless skin seemed to tighten across her high-boned cheeks. "I'll fight you—"

J.D.'s expression hardened, his eyes glittering as they traced her features. "Irish likes me, Kat. You're going to have to swallow this deal down your beautiful throat."

"I intend to get Irish out of this mess," she said in a voice that send an ache rippling through him. Suddenly he wanted her to need him. But Katherine's pride would never allow it.

He noted again the fast-beating pulse at the base of her throat. He longed to take her long, smooth neck between his two hands, to feel that pulse flutter beneath his thumbs. He wanted to feel the hot blood she kept so carefully hidden wash to the surface, and then maybe, just maybe he'd be able to walk away. Because he could at least feel her hatred, he added his special torment. "You'll have to deal with me this time, Kat. Irish doesn't know a thing about you and me—how it really was back then. And she was in a hell of a mess."

Her shoulders straightened slowly, as though she was fighting deep fatigue. "I can imagine. You stepped in the moment she needed you, of course. You wouldn't miss the chance for an attractive acquisition. But you won't get near her," she finished quietly.

"You're not jealous, are you, Angel? Of me and Irish?" he prodded, feeling the quiet rage stalk him once more. "Denver's Avenging Angel—if they only knew their angel had a dollar sign for her heart. Our reunion—via Irish—should be interesting."

He leaned forward, watching her absorb his contempt. She needed to know every minute particle of his revenge and more. "You know, Kat, you remind me of King Arthur's sword, Excalibur. It took just the right man to withdraw the embedded blade from the rock—"

She paled visibly, and J.D. registered again the thrust of her bones beneath the tight skin. Momentarily he allowed himself to be concerned about her, a habit he thought he'd forgotten. "Kat, you're looking damn fragile. What's wrong with you?"

He leaned closer, inspecting her face closely. "The fact that you can't control this situation has really gotten under your skin, hasn't it?"

Katherine refused to move back, feeling his heat penetrate her clothing, slide against her bare flesh. The scent of expensive after-shave wafted to her and she hated it. It barely shielded his personal scent, one she didn't want to remember. She wondered briefly if he still wore his talisman, the Indian stone, beneath his shirt.

The thought of his good-luck charm evoked a memory she wanted to forget. She could still see the talisman, nestled in the dark hair covering his chest and feel it warmed by the heat of their lovemaking, the sheen of their damp bodies blending on the dark green stone.

She'd felt it press hard into her naked breast as he'd moved over her that first time, easing into her with a gentle control that had made her love him even more.

He'd seen the stone lying against her pale skin and had lifted it from his neck. His mouth had rubbed the tender impression it had left behind, the heat flowing wildly between them as she slowly accepted him.

Murmuring words of endearment, encouraging her to meet him, trembling in her shy arms, J.D. had been the perfect first lover.

She'd let him love her, welcoming him deep within her heart! Katherine trembled, fighting her reaction to his nearness. What a fool she'd been.

She couldn't let Irish make the same mistake....

Forcing herself to block out the memory of the primitive leather thong and the dull green stone lying upon his dark chest, Katherine met his eyes evenly.

She had never wasted time hating, but looking at J.D. now, she experienced the full depth of the emotion. "How much?" she clipped out, feeling her muscles tense as he rose to stand over her.

Looking down at her, J.D.'s features were all rugged angles, lacking even a centimeter of softness. The decor of his offices—starkly masculine—suited him, she decided. His jaw bore a day's growth of beard, the cords of muscle moving rhythmically beneath his dark skin. His blue dress shirt was unbuttoned at the neck, hair escaping the wedge. The soft fabric clung to his broad shoulders and lean body. Katherine swallowed the dry wadding that seemed suddenly to lodge in her throat and looked out at the night.

She could feel him breathe, sense him watching the fluttering pulse at the base of her throat. Then unexpectedly his fingers were in her hair, forcing her to her feet.

Katherine lifted her face to him, arranging her expression into the cool mask that was one of the marks of her style. She forced her hands to stillness at her sides, knowing his strength. She could feel the power throbbing from him, the muscles ready; he was expecting her to fight.

She refused to give him what he wanted. Now or ever.

His fingers rubbed at the tension in her neck with an easy strength. It was as though he liked having her within his grasp. "It's just you and me, one-on-one," he murmured huskily. "The good guys and the bad guys."

He tipped back her face, examining it at leisure. "You're scared this time, aren't you, Kat? Really afraid of my relationship to Irish," he murmured almost to himself.

"The cost, J.D.," Katherine insisted quietly, watching the growing excitement flicker in his eyes. Her stomach contracted when his gaze touched her mouth and lingered, heating.

His fingers sifted through her hair, letting the strands drift free as though he savored the texture. He crushed the ends, studying the various shades in the dim light. His warm breath stroked her cheek and she felt herself shudder. J.D.

moved his hand, resting the rough palm lightly against her jaw. "What's in there, Kat?" he asked thoughtfully. "Woman or machine? Where did you bury the laughing girl?"

His thumb lightly brushed her bottom lip and he narrowed his eyes. "Exactly how much is Irish worth to you, Kat?"

The intimate, insinuating tone stroked icy chills down her back. Katherine wrenched free, facing him, her body taut with the urge to physically lash out at him. "Is this the place where I offer myself in lieu of my sister?"

Katherine regretted the verbal attack instantly—almost. If J.D. could play rough, so could she. But she wanted him to back off. He could terrify her when he got too close, and she'd learned how to go for the heart when she was scared.

Straightening her shoulders, she lifted her head. He'd asked for a fight, he could damn well have it.

"You're tired and on a knife-point, Kat," he drawled after a long moment. He tilted his head arrogantly. "Do I do that to you?"

J.D. was pushing, prowling around her, sensing where to land the next blow. She could feel him gauging just how far to take the moment. A show of temper was something Katherine never allowed herself, but at that moment she began to wonder if she could handle any situation involving J. D. MacLean. He was entirely too close, disturbing her emotions. She felt her legs weakening, as though she were being unraveled a piece at a time. More huskily than she intended, Katherine stated her demand. "I want this farce ended tonight."

"This time the ball is in my court, sweet Katherine," he returned easily. "The way I see the whole situation is this. Without declaring Irish incompetent to handle her own affairs, there isn't a thing you can do about our partnership. You're at my mercy," he added pleasantly.

Her throat contracted suddenly as J.D.'s dark eyes flicked across her mouth. "How was it—" he asked darkly, as though the words were forcibly drawn from him "—making love with a man twenty years older than you? Spending his money and laughing at the poor, sweating trucker?"

She'd expecting nothing less from J.D. He hadn't the slightest idea about her relationship with Big Jim, how he'd let her make her own choices—talked them over with her. J.D. hadn't given her an ounce of trust when he'd had the chance. He had to snatch all the decisions into his own big fist—just as he was trying to do now.

"Big Jim was my husband—"

"Damn it. I don't want to hear about him now," he declared roughly, and she caught the first glimpse of his dark, savage anger. She licked her lips nervously and found him staring at them almost hungrily. "Not now."

"I don't have to take this," she managed unevenly as he ran a fingertip across her damp lips. She felt herself tremble at his touch and hated her reaction. All J.D. needed to make himself happy was to see her lose her famous control. And at the moment it had all the lasting strength of a soggy cobweb in a high wind. He'd taunted her with her lack of frailty, but right now she had her share. He'd howl with delight.

"No, you wouldn't want to take it. But by God, I do," he rasped, then his mouth covered hers.

Somehow she was caught in his arms, emotions swirling about them like a flooding stream.

Katherine braced herself against the expected savagery of his mouth, her opened hands pressing against the solid planes of his chest. But his lips touched lightly, brushing hers, savoring...

His large hands framed her face, lifting her mouth to his easy, tantalizing kisses. His lips were soft, with the flavor of hers. She breathed lightly, realizing that he held her gently, without hurting.

His heart pounded savagely beneath her open palm. A tremor ran the length of his long, taut body, and something like fear exploded in her, catching her by the throat. When the movement lifted her softness to his chest, he hesitated, running one hand around to span her back.

J.D. drew her nearer, breathing hard against her cheek. "It's going to be finished this time, Kat. You can bet on it," he whispered roughly.

He shuddered then, running his open hand slowly back and forth across her back, easing her against him. When Katherine looked up, she saw his eyes softly drift shut, a frown between his thick brows, as though he were concentrating—on her?

She didn't want to feel the warmth melting her body. She didn't want to lift her mouth to his again, nor offer the slow, sweet kiss that followed as if all those years had never happened.

She didn't want to respond to him on any level. But the drugging kisses deepened, his teeth catching her lower lip and nibbling gently around the soft perimeter. Fighting the sensual mists, she turned her head away from those seeking lips, feeling them brush her hot cheek. "J.D., I came here for a business conference, and you're forcibly restraining me without my permission."

"Really?" he drawled, kissing her eyelids one at a time. "Then give me permission, Kat."

She shivered, fighting the romantic background of Mancini and the impulse to slide her hand down his chest, exploring the flat, muscled stomach. "You can go—"

J.D. was watching her closely now. He ran his hand down the length of her back and smiled a smile that made her very skin seem to ripple. As though conducting an experiment, he slowly repeated the movement.

Katherine unwillingly closed her eyes, wrapped in the sheer sensation of being feminine, a woman with a man. She'd needed that through the years, she realized. Now the emotion curled around her like a sweet, erotic spice.

She sensed that her body was waiting for his returning touch, felt her breasts surge slightly beneath the satin—

"You're trembling, Kat," he murmured against her ear.

As though she were his intimate, very special experiment. "It's amazing how soft you are, how slender...."

J.D.'s hand stroked her shoulders, easing the taut muscles there. It continued to stroke, to knead, to caress as she watched him helplessly. In some tiny, sane portion of her brain, she recognized her first mistake—approaching J.D. when she was bone tired and nervous as a cat on ice. His touch ran down the length of her satin-covered arm, his fingers testing the fine bones of her wrist. Then he turned her palm upward, circling the soft pads with his thumb.

Stirring, Katherine moved slightly against him, desperately trying to leash the subtle, no longer dormant ache within her. The scent of his skin seemed to wrap itself around her as his lips followed the taut length of her neck upward to taste her earlobe. "Don't worry about Irish, Katherine," he murmured there. "She'll be fine."

Irish. The name sliced through the warm sensuality like a hot blade on butter. Katherine's half-closed eyes widened as J.D.'s parted lips followed a taut cord down her throat.

Absolutely still within his arms, Katherine recognized her own rising panic. Was this how J.D. had held or intended to hold her sister?

Thrusting against his chest, Katherine forced herself free and faced him, her mind whirling, fighting a savage anger. She'd felt a sharp jolt of deep jealousy, had recognized it instantly and resented it. She shivered as she watched J.D.'s gaunt face harden, a hot flush rising beneath the dark tan. "Save that approach for someone else, and I don't mean Irish," she ordered curtly.

J.D.'s eyes glittered; now he wrapped the sheer force of his anger around her. "You're not jealous, are you, Angel?" he asked again, too softly.

"Hardly. I've had better." Turning her back, Katherine walked toward the door on shaking legs.

She paused as her hand touched the cool knob and J.D.'s deep voice snared her. "Until we meet again, Angel."

* * *

Katherine kicked the twisted sheets away from her legs and glanced at her bedside clock. At two o'clock in the morning she hated J. D. MacLean more than she ever had in her life.

He would never get to her again.

He wouldn't have come close to catching her by surprise if she hadn't been so exhausted and on edge.

Maybe she really did need that vacation at Irish's. She definitely needed to talk sense to her sister and pull her out of J.D.'s clutches. Katherine sighed. In the morning she'd start making plans to share her work load with her other associates. Taking time off to vacation wouldn't be easy, but she definitely needed rest to handle J.D.

Had he held Irish, looked at her with that hot, glittering hunger?

Katherine punched her pillow. At the thought of J.D. near Irish, she got steamed up all over again. Flopping to her stomach, she gripped the brass posts of her bed until her hands ached. She was mad at herself, of course, for allowing him to raise her emotions so easily. In the future she'd have to keep J.D. away from her and on a business course.

Forcing herself to release the bedposts finger by finger, Katherine willed herself to sleep. She needed every bit of strength she had to talk Irish into letting her buy out J.D.

And she needed every dram of strength to knock J.D. back into the past where he belonged.

She didn't want to feel anything when it came to J. D. MacLean.

Three

————

Two weeks later, Katherine arrived in Kodiak to start her first minivacation. She intended to have several, catching up on much-needed rest and using the time to retrieve her baby sister from J.D.'s dubious clutches.

A typical Western "wide spot in the road," Kodiak's business section consisted of a single gas station. The truck stop café with a grocery store and a few scattered houses completed the town. Anyone needing a post office stopped by the gas station.

Irish's bed-and-breakfast stood back from the main highway, all cornices and wide porches and high peaked roofs. The main roof slanted questionably, while the rest of the house seemed to ramble out at angles. The inn resembled a grand old lady wrapped in lace and rocking in the foothills of the rugged Rocky Mountains.

At the height of the Colorado silver-mining boom the rambling white house had served as a classy bordello and

gambling hall, its well-known madame, Abagail Whitehouse, killed in a struggle between her two lovers.

Irish Dalton loved the place, from its notorious past to its
restored, antique furniture. Aided by an ancient woman
called Granny, whose roots were deep in Colorado's history, Irish babied the house's disreputable plumbing and
sloping floors. A man even older than Granny "tinkered"
the plumbing into working order and supervised transient
and schoolboy labor. This odd mixture of young and old
cared for the hundred acres that stretched beyond the house
and into the rising mountains.

For Katherine, the house meant a continual awareness of
her major problem: legally, J. D. MacLean owned her
younger sister.

That fact had gnawed at Katherine all night despite her
sumptuous, ornate quarters. The huge, walnut four-poster
bed and matching, carved dresser had been salvaged from
the original furniture of the bordello. In the year since Irish
had installed herself in the house, Katherine had poured
herself onto the restored bed several times, soaking up its
elegant luxury. There was something about wriggling her
bare toes against the sun-dried sheets that cast her courtroom skirmishes into oblivion.

But this morning—just weeks after meeting J.D. at the
airport—Katherine felt listless and tired. She was no more
rested than when she had arrived here at dusk the previous
day.

Now, seated in her sister's big, bright country kitchen,
Katherine badly needed a magic spell to understand Irish's
bookkeeping system. It involved a cookie jar shaped like an
apple and a size-five shoe box. The apple was for big bills,
Irish explained cheerily, the box for smaller ones. Katherine nodded, grimly eyeing the stamp J.D. had given Irish.
His personal signature stood behind any bills for the bed-
and-breakfast.

The legal document Irish had extracted from an old food
tin was a copy of her partnership agreement with J.D.

Katherine had to admit that it appeared to be binding and absolutely without loopholes.

Beyond the kitchen, a reconditioned MacLean shuttle van glittered ominously in the June sun. How like him, she thought, to leave reminders of his possession.

Irish smiled and adjusted a ruffled calico curtain against the bright, morning sun, her short, blond hair catching fiery red sparks. "How about another cup of morning go-juice, Kat? You look so—" she smiled impishly "—ghostly."

Irish never failed to try to breathe life into Abagail Whitehouse's ghostly presence, and Katherine smiled in spite of herself. "Irish, you know there is no ghost here."

"Of course there is, if we work with the idea. People love the idea of a resident ghost. It'll be a great sales pitch. Romantic, too. From the looks of you, you could use a little fantasy."

"Thanks a lot." Katherine ached to snatch up the partnership agreement and toss it into the garbage. "Do you have any idea—?"

With her loving heart and bubbly personality, Irish considered major problems as though they were gnats. Dressed today in a red T-shirt, jeans and sneakers, she looked like a teenager. Irish took a deep, fortifying breath—the one she always took before accusing Katherine of "nibbling minor details to death."

Katherine closed her eyes, picturing J.D.'s slow, deadly grin. He had just the right, sensuous look to belong in this hundred-and-twenty-year-old "entertainment palace." She could easily picture him dressed in gambler's black, with a scarlet garter about his upper arm, a cigar clenched between his white teeth as he eyed the possible "doves."

Why think about him now? Because she was deeply tired and off balance. Her control right now was dubious, Katherine acknowledged, hating her weakness and the knowledge that it could cost people who trusted her. With trembling fingers she adjusted the long, cream satin robe over her knees as Irish poured coffee.

Irish stepped back and eyed her critically. "How about some biscuits and gravy, honey?"

"No, thanks. I'd have to spend a week in the gym to get rid of the pounds."

"You're too thin, Kat. All bones and big eyes. You look worse than you did when Big Jim died. Must be the work-aholic diet. Here, at least have an apple." Irish reached into the overflowing fruit bowl. "You look like you're about to go over the edge. Taking on too many defenseless souls, fighting for injustice and all that?"

Katherine couldn't help grinning as she took a bite of the crisp, green apple. To protect the innocent had been a childhood dream of hers. "Irish, we do have to talk," she said as Irish sat down on one of the antique chairs.

"I recognize the older-sister-giving-advice tone, Kat. I thought you were vacationing. You've got that wired look, as though you're stoking up for a good fight."

Katherine riffled through a mound of bills all stamped with J.D.'s bold signature. "Why did you have to go to him, Irish? I've offered more than once—"

Irish looked at her, raising her chin in the characteristic Dalton fighting gesture. "I'm twenty-seven," she reminded her sister firmly. "After Mark and I broke up, all I had was a degree in home economics and five years of fil-ing experience at the bank. I need this, Kat. And I can't al-low you to interfere. I had a little savings, and the bank loaned me the rest—J.D. refinanced the loan or something when he started helping me. I intend to make it work. We're making it work," she corrected herself.

Placing one hand on her waist, she continued. "So what if I'm having a rough patch? You've had plenty of them, and you survived. Look at when Big Jim died five years ago and you had to fight the entire board of trustees—"

"Big Jim taught me a lot of things, Irish. You walked into this bed-and-breakfast with no idea—"

"So who are you, anyway? I had my dreams, Kat. Everyone has dreams, and nothing happens without them.

You wanted to be a lawyer and now you are." Irish frowned. "Okay, so I'm not great at adding up numbers. I *am* good at taking care of people. I give them a piece of home."

She looked earnestly at Katherine. "People need that homey feeling, Kat. Don't you ever feel that way? Like you need someone taking care of you?"

Lately Katherine had been feeling just that way, she admitted reluctantly. She'd seen too much, thrown herself into her salvation campaigns, and it had nearly cost her health. But she would survive; it was Irish who concerned her right now. "That's not what I'm saying. You've done a beautiful job here. But J.D.—"

Irish turned on her like a cat defending her kitten. "J.D. has been wonderful. We're partners, Kat."

"Partners?" Katherine swirled the word around carefully, watching her sister. Was she aware of what J.D. could do to her as a woman? Of the sleepless nights and slashing anger? Irish was an innocent compared to J.D., and now they were partners. The word started a mental avalanche, bringing to mind all sorts of possible disasters. "Irish, J.D. has a reputation—"

"Partners," Irish interrupted blithely. "Like Dale and Roy. Like Chip and Dale. J.D. is handling the business part, while I manage the inn. People have business managers every day. Our preholiday charity bash is going to make history in the bed-and-breakfast catalogs," she went on excitedly. "He's working on brochures right now and—"

"I want to know," Katherine interjected grimly, "exactly how and when you got under J.D.'s thumb."

"Don't you take that tone of voice with me, Miss Katherine," Irish told her lightly after a tense moment. "I'm your sister, remember. Not the chief suspect in some heinous crime."

"Irish, J. D. MacLean is—" Katherine began hotly, only to be stilled by a slashing look.

"My friend," Irish finished the sentence. "I swear, you workaholics can be depressing when it comes to fun and friendship. What you need is someone to make you relax."

Irish paused, studying Katherine carefully; too carefully, the older woman realized. "Lighten up, Kat," she added softly. "What if the right guy comes along and you're in one of those sic'em moods? You'll scare him away."

Acknowledging that Irish had chosen her path and wouldn't back up an inch, Katherine looked away, turning her eyes to the mountains, suddenly feeling very worn. Why hadn't she realized how tired she was, how vulnerable?

Irish sighed, then went on. "An admirable quality, Kat. Carrying the world on your shoulders. But you know, if I could change one thing about you, that would be it. Sometime you're going to have to let go—give a little slice of yourself to someone else. Let someone else—oh, don't give me that patiently suffering look. When did you really enjoy anything but a good courtroom brawl?"

Irish leaned closer, her expression concerned. "I hope I didn't hurt your feelings, Kat. It's just that this was something I had to do on my own. You would have taken over. You've got a habit of doing that.... You dissect things, take the romance and the adventure out of them," she said, nervously twisting a sponge. "Kat, you've made your mistakes. I need to make mine, too. The why and the how of J.D. and me becoming partners isn't really important, is it?"

Katherine knew that why's and how's were extremely important when dealing with J.D. A cold chill ran down her spine. She sipped the scalding coffee, barely feeling the burn on her tongue. Then straightening her shoulders and taking a deep breath, she made a promise to herself: she'd straighten out her life, find her needs and recapture her health. And while she was doing that, if there was a loophole in J.D.'s scheme to acquire Irish, she'd find it, too.

Later, dressed in jeans, boots and a bulky, blue sweater, Katherine walked to the stables with Irish. Rio, J.D.'s stallion, grazed in a meadow, another reminder of his hold on

Irish. The barn itself sheltered a mare, four aged donkeys—
which, Irish swore, were descended from early Colorado
mining stock—and one bony mule, another of her bar-
gains.

Katherine lifted her face to the breeze. Its cold touch carried scents of new green fields and sprawling forest land. She
needed that simplicity. "This is a great place. Though I've
only seen two elderly couples for guests, they were holding
hands and laughing like kids."

Irish grinned as she looped her arm through Katherine's.
"You just wait until next year. We'll be filled to the brim.
J.D. thinks we should change the name to Abagail's—
something that would play up the resident madame ghost
idea. She'd be a great marketing tool, he said."

Katherine lifted a rotten board to toss it aside. She wished
she could get J.D. out of her path as easily. She shot a glance
at the cottage the madame was said to have used for her
private amours. "I suppose he likes the painting of the re-
clining lady with the skimpy scarf?"

Irish tugged at her hair. "You could take a few lessons
from her. They say Abagail LaRue Whitehouse liked to
laugh a lot. I've got the feeling you last laughed about two
centuries ago. Her things are still in the camelback trunk in
your room. You'd look great in them."

"Why on earth would I want to try on your resident
ghost's clothing?"

Irish's grin was positively wicked. "You've gotten moldy,
that's why. It might give you some ideas. They say sex is a
great outlet. A necessary drive. Maybe that's why the
honeymooners like Abagail. So did J.D. He said she was
quite a woman."

"J.D. can go hang," Katherine announced hotly before
she realized she had spoken. "Of course, he'd like the bordello idea—and you can stop thinking right now that I'm a
frustrated widow."

"You're hardly the merry widow, Kat. Come on, try on
Abagail's clothes. It'll be fun."

Irish gave her apple core to Morticia, the mule. "You can be just like a tough little snail, you know, huddling in your shell."

Irish reached through the corral boards to pat a mare whose spine curved low in the middle. "Kat, I know you've got your back up about J.D.'s ... about our partnership."

"I still want to know how you two—" Katherine began, wondering if Irish really knew which sister J.D. had placed on his masculine menu.

Irish lifted one finger and two eyebrows. "Stop."

While Katherine dealt with her aching ulcer and the thought that J.D. could be turning up at any time, Irish reached up to kiss her cheek. "Don't worry so, Kat. It makes lines."

Katherine tried desperately to retreat to the soothing mental image of her private, rippling stream. The stream had dried up. She heard herself groan.

Irish smoothed her hair. "Poor Kat. You really do need rest. You're such a worrywart. But I'll take care of everything, including you."

That night Katherine adjusted a cool, damp cloth across her forehead as she laid her head on the satin pillowcase. She stared at the ceiling chandelier, which seemed to sway gently, its long crystals glittering in the candlelight.

Her room retained its original opulent red velvet and carved oak flavor. A giant, claw-footed tub sat behind Oriental screens. She caught just the faintest scent of lavender and a heavier musk and groaned. The laughing, sexy madame and herself had nothing in common.

Katherine turned the cold compress, closed her eyes and groaned again.

"It's just the second week of June. We can still plant a field of wildflowers in that weed patch over there," Irish said, sweeping the wide front porch with her broom. She glanced at her sister's thoughtful profile. The Colorado sun highlighted her blond hair. Katherine always was a sight in

blue jeans and a sweatshirt, Irish decided. Like it or not,
J.D.'s dark, exciting looks were a perfect foil for Katherine's cool, leggy beauty.

It would be interesting to see the two of them together—
if her plan worked. There was just something thunderous
about Katherine whenever Irish mentioned J.D.'s name.
"My, you're deep in thought, Kat. I bet you haven't heard
a word of my plans."

"Mmm?" Katherine turned to her sister, brushing a
strand of hair from her cheek. Running the back of her
hand across her throat, Katherine once more felt his parted
lips caress her skin as though tasting it. The touch had been
gentle, almost sweet. She breathed sharply, slowly expel-
ling the air. It was impossible. Men like J.D. had steel suits
of armor for skin and blocks of concrete for hearts. When
he touched a woman, he had an immediate need—

"It must be living in a bordello," Katherine muttered,
dusting a clinging leaf from her jeans.

"A former bordello," Irish stated firmly.

Katherine grinned and stretched, inhaling the clean,
country air. "What were you saying about flowers?"

"I want peonies—miles of 'em. And by the way, I really
do believe that Abagail LaRue Whitehouse still inhabits the
house."

"Irish, stop that. The place is old. There isn't a level
board in it. The foundation is weak and allows things to
bounce. Whatever else happens is due to gravity, not ghost.
You put packets of lavender around the house last night.
You're actively promoting Abagail."

Irish sniffed haughtily. "She'd have a perfect excuse not
to leave this world entirely. Imagine, throwing herself between two lovers, taking the bullets so they could live—"

"Abagail was a madame, Irish," Katherine corrected,
watching a small boy playing with a frisky puppy that was
dancing through the high weeds in the field near Abagail's
infamous cottage. The boy's black, straight hair shone in the

morning sunlight as the shaggy puppy ran circles around him.

She ran the flat of her hand across the emptiness in her stomach. She'd wanted J.D.'s children once. The month had been endless after they had made love.... She shrugged, putting the thought behind her just as she had through the years. "I'll check on the brownies. And then we've got to talk about J.D.," she repeated for the fifth time in three days.

"He suits me," Irish stated flatly. "We're partners, and I won't have you lying in wait for him as if he were some sleazy carpetbagger. Honestly, Kat, you've got to stop looking at everyone's intentions as though they just wanted to make money. J.D. said this place is a real challenge—just the sort of thing he's been looking for. He's not an evil person, you know, Kat," she declared hotly.

She flounced off the porch toward the small boy, then turned back to Katherine. "Not another word, Kat. I mean it."

Katherine took one long look at Irish's set face and decided she'd have better luck with her brownies.

Just when the aroma of freshly baked brownies had thoroughly scented the house, a crash sounded at the back door. Katherine heard the small boy's voice give a hushed scolding to his puppy. The puppy yelped louder as the boy tried to quiet him. Opening the door, she saw an overturned chair.

The little boy blinked his long, straight lashes innocently. He tugged at his sagging, dirty jeans.

Katherine bent down to him. He had a solemn look, watching her with guarded, black eyes. "My name is Katherine," she said gently. "And who are you?"

He reached out to hold the shaggy puppy against his leg. "Travis. He's Puddles."

Katherine opened the door to the kitchen. "I'm getting ready to frost brownies. Would you like to help me, Travis?"

"Uh-huh."

Smiling, Katherine waited; the boy steadily returned her gaze. "I'm Irish's sister, Travis. My mother called me Kat," she offered. Travis held tight to the puppy. "It will be all right. You can come in."

Walking past her, his puppy following, Travis turned and stood in the kitchen. Uncertainty flickered in his eyes. "I don't have a mommy or a daddy. They're in heaven," he said. "But I have Grandpa."

Katherine felt her heart turn flip-flops and warm to the boy. "I'll bet your grandpa would love some brownies, Travis. If you help me, I'll send some home for him," she suggested, pointing to the kitchen sink. "Just stand on that stool to wash your hands. Then you can—"

Travis clasped his hands behind him. "Don't like soap."

Smiling, Katherine leaned over to kiss his cheek. The boy slowly raised his hand to cover the spot, still watching her with wide, dark eyes. "Travis, washing hands is one of my rules." Katherine picked up the mixing bowl containing the fudge frosting and stirred it temptingly. "You could lick the bowl later."

Minutes later his clean hands reached for the wooden spoon. His small tongue escaped as he studiously swirled the back of the spoon across the dessert. Katherine glanced at the boy while she cut the finished brownies into squares. There was just something cuddly about him. As though he needed someone to hold him.

Children had needs, she thought, watching him. And she still had to discover hers as an adult.

Placing a brownie on his napkin, she straightened his coal-black hair gently. There was just something.... Travis's black eyes watched her quietly, intently. "You kiss like Mommy did," he whispered shyly. "I miss Mommy and Daddy."

Because she had to, Katherine kissed him again, nuzzling his cheek affectionately. "Well, you have me now, Travis.

And anytime you want a mommy kiss, you come see me, okay?''

He nodded. After his second brownie Travis commented, "Good. Can I take some home to Grandpa?''

"You sure can." She found herself automatically straightening his wayward hair again. "Do you want to tell me about your grandpa?''

"Yep." His black eyes went wide, looking up at her. "Sometimes I cry at night and Grandpa holds me. Grandpa's never going to let nothing happen to me."

Irish snapped the cotton top sheet as she made Travis's bed in the madame's small cottage. She glanced at J.D., who was arranging the air pump for a small tank of guppies. "Kat is not hard-hearted," she contested. "She's over at the house now, baking brownies with Travis. If she were as totally cold as you say, she wouldn't have anything to do with children."

Irish shook her head, wondering how two such perfectly matched people could be so stubborn when it came to each other. It was truly fate that had caused J.D.'s car to break down near her inn last December, she thought. On their way home from Daisy and her husband's funeral, he and Travis were two sorry, needing souls, and she had enjoyed taking care of them. When J.D. left, he'd extended a sincere offer to help her if she needed him. She had.

But the financial thing was just a dull dip in the chop suey, she'd decided later. The real meat at the end of the chopstick was that by allowing J.D. to help her, she could take care of him and Travis.

And she could…well, play matchmaker between J.D. and Katherine. Lately Katherine had been worrying her. With her nose so firmly to the legal grindstone, she could never have fun. It would take someone equally strong to draw her out of her shell.

That was where J.D. fitted into Irish's plans. She knew they were perfect for each other. They just needed a little nudging....

So Irish had called J.D. and asked for help.

Her unwary victim straightened slowly, wiping his hands on a towel and lifting a brow at Irish. "You two are as different as night and day. If Kat is baking brownies, it's because that's the only way she can get them."

Irish placed her hands on her hips. "Okay, smart guy. Explain this—I was just about to enter the house when I saw her hugging and kissing Travis. He needs a lot of that, you know. If she's so insensitive, so cold-hearted, why did she do it? What's her motive?"

Throwing down the towel, J.D. scowled at her. "How should I know?"

He glanced at the inn. So Katherine had it in her to hug and kiss Travis, did she?

Suddenly, unwillingly he remembered the soft, caring way she'd tended Daisy. A kiss on a tiny scratch or a bruised knee. He pictured her falling asleep in the old rocker as she held Daisy on her lap, her lips softly parted and just waiting—

God, she could make him ache. J.D. rubbed his jaw, still feeling as raw and restless as he had all the years without Katherine.

Travis needed whatever love and attention he could get. If Katherine could wring some tenderness out of herself for the boy, J.D. was grudgingly grateful.

"You give her a chance, J.D.," Irish ordered firmly from behind him. "She's not too happy about our partnership, and I don't want to give her any more problems than she already has."

"The only problem that woman has is—"

"Be careful. She's family, J.D., and I won't have you badmouthing her. She's someone I love and can count on," Irish said.

Tactfully changing the subject then, she asked, "So you really think we can market this Going-to-Grandma's sort of theme to stressed-out executives? It's one of my better ideas, I think. That and the health spa and mud bath."

J.D.'s expression lost its dark, closed-in look and he began to grin reluctantly. Irish punched his arm. "Let 'er rip, partner. I want to hear your ideas about reviving our madame ghost."

Travis sipped his milk, licking his tongue across the white mustache on his upper lip. He studied Katherine for a long moment, then reached his chubby hand toward her hair. "Pretty. Like Mommy's," he commented softly.

She laughed and hugged him. "I hope your grandpa likes the brownies."

Travis locked his arms around her neck and Katherine kissed his cheek, rocking him gently. After a moment, the boy carefully lifted his grandfather's plate of brownies from the counter. Katherine smiled at the idea of a tottering old man besieged by a small boy and a dog named Puddles. She riffled Travis's hair. "I imagine I'll be making more later this week. You check back, okay?"

"Uh-huh." The door slammed behind the pair.

For the next hour Katherine looked through the worldly possessions of Madame Whitehouse while she waited for Irish. Stuffed in the old camelback trunk, the array of black corsets, garters and hose still held the scent of an erotic perfume. Two beautiful, Chinese silk wrappers embroidered with red and black dragons were neatly folded beneath a long, black silk chemise. The scent drifted about Katherine's room, lingering as she placed the garments on her bed. She spread a carved ivory fan decorated with tassels, enjoying its Oriental beauty. The phone rang downstairs.

When she answered it, the raw baritone on the other end of the line froze her in place. "Kat? J.D."

"Yes?" She wished she hadn't sounded so breathless. "What do you want?" she asked flatly.

He was quiet a moment, then answered slowly, "You wouldn't want to know, Kat."

The sensuous drawl set her off like flame applied to a dried pinecone. "J.D., you leave Irish alone. She just barely got back on her feet after Mark. I forbid you to—"

"Why, Kat. You're a little late. I've got big plans for Irish."

Katherine was so angry that she could feel her toes warm within her sneakers. "I'm here now, J.D. Anything you have to discuss with Irish, you can discuss with me first."

He laughed then, that husky, I've-got-you laugh that sent chills rippling down her spine. "Just how long can you leave your practice to protect your baby sister?" he asked mockingly.

"Where are you?" she asked suddenly, needing to place him at a safe distance. Enemies like MacLean needed to be red-pegged on a big map marked Danger Zone.

"Tell Irish I called, will you, Kat?" he asked, and then the line went dead. Katherine slammed down the receiver, wishing she could wrap the cord around J.D.'s well-muscled neck.

By early evening she had fed the stock and painted the white picket fence twice. She needed the clean, spring air to wash away the memory of J.D.'s husky laughter. Working furiously had helped to ease her temper; now, as a personal gift to herself, she filled the claw-footed, antique tub to the brim with expensive, French bubble bath.

To soothe her chafed nerves Katherine lighted scented candles, bathing her room in a soft glow.

She slipped into the fragrant, sudsy depths with a long sigh just as the telephone rang again downstairs. A moment later the stairway creaked beneath her sister's slight weight. Irish knocked on the door and asked, "Kat, are you decent?"

"No. What is it?" Katherine scooped a mound of bubbles across her throat to form a necklace.

"The honeymooners checked out, and I've got to run over to the cottage," Irish called, and then her footsteps sounded again.

The large, two-story house groaned, settling for the night. The antique water heater, straining to refill itself with hot water, knocked and clattered like old bones. One of the shutters banged as the wind whistled around the corners of the house. The loosened wood shingles rattled, and the branch of a tall fir tree scraped the elegant, stained glass at Katherine's window.

A coyote howled in the distance, the sound forbidding. The wind rose and the tasseled shade covering the window flapped up. The glass chandelier overhead trembled slightly, the long tiers rattling almost musically.

"Okay, Abagail," Katherine murmured, stepping out of the tub to dry herself. "You can stop rattling your bones now. I'm done with my bath."

She glanced at the large, four-poster bed and the antique garments strewn across it. "I wonder...."

The flimsy, ruffled black lace chemise slid down her body, clearly outlining the curves of her breasts. Katherine drew on the black silk drawers with the tiny, intriguing, red bows, then fitted the black lace corset around her waist. She held her breath, straining to tug the laces tighter beneath her bosom. "This outfit would really match my briefcase and pumps," Katherine said aloud, laughing as she reached for the black silk hose and ruffled red garters.

The sleek silk, topped by the red satin, encased her legs with elegance.

Katherine caught her reflection in the standing, oval mirror. Lifting a small box from the trunk, she opened it—to find tortoise shell hairpins, long, jet eardrops and a red silk rose.

She wistfully arranged her hair in an upward style, anchoring the strands with the long pins. Fascinated by the personal items of this woman from a bygone age, Katherine slid the earrings into place and tucked the rose into her hair.

The madame's musky scent lingered as Katherine tilted her head, studying the long-legged, sexy image intently. With her hair piled high, and dressed to incite a masculine riot, she looked nothing like Denver's cool, avenging angel now.

She touched the curve of her left breast experimentally above the skimpy black lace. Lifted higher by the laced corset, her softness peeked through the lace like pale satin.

Running the tip of one finger across the frilly bodice, she tried to think of Big Jim and his gentleness. Katherine tilted her head and the earrings glittered in the candlelight. When they'd made love it had been like a sweet caress, and she'd enjoyed his undemanding touch. They'd been friends—had respected each other—and somehow sensuality had never been at the center of their marriage.

Maybe she'd been too busy. But they'd both been happy... hadn't they?

Big Jim had always been gentle and he had trusted her. Unlike J.D.

Running her fingertip across her lips, she remembered J.D.'s uneven breathing, his body locked hard against hers. J.D. wouldn't know how to be gentle....

But when she was eighteen he had been.

Why couldn't he have trusted her to make her own decisions?

She turned sideways, looking over her shoulder at the image in the mirror.

J.D., after all, operated on a base level. How much pleasure it would give her to leave him bleeding—just once. Maybe that was what she needed after all these years. Then maybe she'd have her peace.

Why hadn't she reacted to Big Jim as she had to J.D.? Her feminine senses were almost primitive when J.D. stroked her....

Locked in her thoughts, she heard the door creak open. "What do you think, Irish?" she said, spinning toward the door.

"That's quite an outfit, Angel," J.D. drawled.

Four

Dressed in a faded chambray shirt and worn, snug jeans, J.D. leaned his shoulder against the door frame. Above his crossed arms the shirt gaped and exposed his chest. A leather thong crossed the hair that covered his dark skin.

Remembering that thong and its stone nestled beneath the cloth, her throat went dry. Her hand went to her throat to shield the fast-beating pulse; she remembered the warm press of that stone against her breasts....

The wind howled, scraping a branch against the window.

Speak of the devil and he appears? Think of J.D., and he wanders into her bedroom?

The soles of her feet seemed locked to the Oriental carpet, her flesh chilled. How often through the years had she thought of him like this?—rugged, appealing and about as trustworthy as an avalanche.

The house creaked, protesting its age to the wind.

"Get out." If there was one person she didn't want to see, didn't want to remember, it was J.D.

Lifting one eyebrow, he nodded. "But Kat, I came to see you."

Tired though she was, she could feel her spirit rising, her body gearing for a fight. "How like you to drive down from Denver just to wave your ownership of Irish in my face," she stated flatly, assuming a defensive stance, resting her fists on her waist and digging her nails into her damp palms.

He moved his shoulder against the door frame so that the chambray stretched tightly across his chest. "Just being neighborly," he offered in a sensual drawl. "Did Irish miss the fact that Travis and I are renting Abagail's cottage?"

For a heartbeat Katherine stopped thinking. Irish, it seemed, had a lot to explain, allowing J.D. to move in near her. It was like inviting the wolf to stay at Little Red Riding Hood's house. She wouldn't give him the satisfaction of her surprise as she thought of the little boy's long dark lashes, mirroring J.D.'s. "Travis?"

"You've met him—Daisy's son. I'm his guardian. He's Daisy's son," he repeated softly, and for a moment his grief reached out to Katherine.

As he said the words, the memory of Daisy seemed to dance between them, taking Katherine back to that young time. She could feel the aching memories rushing at her like fallen leaves tossed about by a winter wind.

"I heard about the avalanche. I'm sorry about Daisy," she responded with genuine sympathy. When J.D. continued to look at her, Katherine glanced away. She didn't want to feel anything for him but the undiluted dislike she'd carried for years.

She ached for the child she'd held in her arms and kissed good-night.

"I'm sorry, too," he returned tightly. His gaze flashed down Katherine's costume almost reluctantly, then back up. "I remember coming home and watching you two sleeping on the couch, with the TV playing only a test pattern."

Katherine found herself looking at his eyes; their blackness took her back to that time, when J.D. had bent over her, smoothing Daisy's flyaway hair from her cheek. "Hello, girls," he'd murmured, his expression tender. "Is there any room for me?"

Drowsily she had hooked an arm around his warm neck and the heat between them had started to grow. He'd looked at her mouth with dark, flickering eyes as though he had to taste her or die.

The wind rattled the inn's windows and Katherine moved her eyes, uneasy and hurting badly. She rubbed her upper arms, trying to warm herself as emptiness grew inside her. How like J.D. to start creeping around, stirring up bittersweet memories. "The only way I want to talk to you is over terms. Get out of my room."

Get out of my life. Get out of my mind.

He'd been tracking her emotions, and she hated him for having taken her back in time. Then he smiled. "The brownies were good. Thanks for thinking of me."

She jerked her head back. How could he possibly know just the right words to start her hating him again? she wondered.

"I wouldn't have missed the sight for the world," he continued. "Denver's famous avenging angel all decked out for an evening in the bedroom. Is that how your husband—" he bit off the word "—liked to see you romp around?"

He had that look about him tonight—primitive, living on the edge, waiting for excitement as though nothing could stop him. His dusty boots had long ago lost their shine and, riding low on his hips, a leather belt secured the worn denims. The jeans had the crisp look of mountain sun and cold wind, fitting tightly down the length of his legs.

Without the trappings of his business suit, J.D. looked as though he belonged to the days of cattle drives and gunfighting. Katherine took a step back, glimpsing J.D. at twenty-four once more. The wind had tousled his hair, the strands gleaming as they crossed his forehead. He hadn't shaved and stubble darkened his jaw.

She hadn't seen him like this for years... looking as rugged and timeless as the Rockies outside the house. As cold and as distant. When he smiled, slowly, knowingly, she wanted to launch herself at him. "How dare you?" she began, fighting the urge to reach for the robe that lay on the bed.

Her stomach knotted with tension and she pressed her fingers into her thigh. She wouldn't let J.D. see an ounce of weakness, not a dram, though his gaze swept over her like the slow caress of a lover's hands. Tracing her face and moving downward, J.D.'s stare rested momentarily on her lace-covered breasts, then stole slowly over the length of her legs.

Breathing unevenly now, Katherine nevertheless forced herself to stand still. "If you've seen enough, you can leave."

He smiled, slowly, sensually, with that same heart-riveting masculinity that had tormented her at eighteen. She'd fought the gossips, defied the cautions of her parents to be with him... before he had calmly chosen "what was right" for her.

She resented him in her very marrow...and anger sparked as he continued.

"It's all there—the right equipment—curves, soft, waiting skin. Is that how you... have fun, sweet Kat? By playing like you're a woman who knows all about pleasuring a man? Big Jim was sick a long time before he—"

"Get out of here," Katherine interjected between her teeth.

J.D.'s expression hardened, lines digging into his forehead. Danger swirled about him like a cloud of dust on a hot, dry day just before a summer storm. "When I'm good and ready."

Nodding at her costume, he said, "Angel, if you ever let yourself go, you'll find you didn't need a getup like that. And besides, if you'll remember, I've seen it all before."

J.D. was out for blood. She could scent him tracking, seeking out her weaknesses.

Did he remember the way their bodies had fitted together, how desperately she'd wanted him?

Her throat went dry as she watched the black eyes flicker over her flesh, tasting it, heating it. The too-tight lace chafed at her skin. Nervously, she ran a hand down her thigh, stopping at the satin garter. That reminded her of her costume and its intent—to lure men. Instantly she rubbed her palms together and found them damp. "That's enough."

"Never enough. Not until it's finished. Or has it just begun again? Maybe now is the time to find out.... I won't have my grandson caught between our wars, Kat. Irish is babysitting with Travis, and since we're all four going to be spending time together this summer, maybe now would be a good time to set the ground rules." J.D. moved away from the door, and slowly walked toward her. What she read in his eyes frightened Katherine more than hell itself—it was a man's stark need of a woman.

But she didn't need J.D. touching her, looking at her as though only she could satisfy his hunger.

He paused at her side, his shoulders blocking out the room. A hot tension skittered between them, hovered, then seemed to dive straight into her bones. Sliding a finger down the side of her neck, J.D. tested the beat of her pulse against her flesh. "Why so nervous, Kat?"

Gliding lower, the warm tip of his finger traced her bare shoulders and she shivered. *She wanted to slide her arms around him and never let go.*

She forced the unwanted thought into the night. Not J.D. Never J.D. She'd trusted him once and he'd nearly broken her.

"Damn you," he whispered too softly, the sound quivering through her. "You don't need anyone, do you?" His deep voice lingered, taunting. "Miss Perfect, wrapped in her ivory tower and law books, looking down at the rest of us mortals. You should try examining human frailties, counselor. Maybe invest in one yourself."

Unraveling her piece by piece, he examined the soft trembling of her lips. Her eyes slid from his and their tender, deepening concern. Smoothing her cold cheek, J.D.'s rough fingertips set her aching. "Kat," he whispered huskily; the sound caught at her nerves, sliding warmly over her skin.

She'd fought in courtrooms for years, fought to keep herself free of J.D. for years.

And now he was back—

The door swung shut with a creak and a snap. A second later there was a metallic click as the ancient bolt shot into place. Beyond the door, the key thudded softly as it fell to the Oriental carpeting in the hallway. Watching her, J.D. hesitated, then grinned slowly, unpleasantly. "I guess it's just thee and me, Angel. At least until Irish decides to come looking."

Katherine's blood slowed in her veins, her body chilling again despite the warmth of the room. "Oh, no."

"Oh, yes." Walking past her, J.D. stood next to the bed, studying the carved posters and flounces intently. "What a bed. If only it could talk." With that he sat down and calmly tugged off his boots.

He leaned back against the frilled pillows, crossing his arms behind his head and stretching his long legs over the dainty pattern of the coverlet and her robe.

Katherine tapped her foot, trying to keep down the edge of her temper. "Would you be so kind..."

He chuckled lightly. "I'm too big to slide under the door, honey."

Pressing her lips together, Katherine leveled a dead stare at him. If ever she had wanted to physically attack someone, it was J. D. MacLean. She could feel the sheer need to lash out at him quiver within her like a live thing.

His head turned to study the design in the colored glass window, and Katherine saw J.D.'s lips press into a hard line.

All jutting angles and rough planes covered by weathered skin, his features seemed to thrust at the surface. His quiet, thoughtful expression slipped through her defenses. "This night brings back memories," he murmured—as though he had a heart.

J.D. vulnerable? Impossible. What was it he saw beyond the aged glass?

"I don't care what you—" She didn't want to know any more about him; he was too dangerous to her already. Probing too close to the heart of her, turning over her pain as if it were dry leaves. The memories danced around her like glass beads on a string, the facets changing in the light. "Damn you."

"To hell? Don't bother. I've already been there." Then his expression changed and the lines softened.

"It's like a replay, isn't it?" he asked slowly, sensuously. One dark hand glided down to her cream satin robe, stroking it as though it were her skin. Touching the garment as though he were her lover with every right, J.D. raised it to his face. He rubbed the fine material against his rugged jaw, indulging himself in her scents. The trespass was too intimate, too challenging. And he knew it. Flaunted it before her.

"Wearing that you could be Miss Abagail herself. Entertaining a gentleman caller. Is that what you're really like, Angel? With smoky-gray eyes and soft, trembling lips and a body that would feel like silk in a man's hands?"

While Katherine struggled to find the appropriate condemning and scathing statement, J.D. deftly whipped off his leather belt. He tossed it onto a chair and snuggled his head into the down pillows, obviously making himself comfortable on her bed. "I've always wondered about this bedroom.... Why don't you take down your hair. That would add a nice touch."

Katherine could feel the strain as anger rippled through her. She took a deep breath—then regretted it instantly, as

J.D.'s gaze immediately swept to the crevice between her breasts.

She tugged the lace higher, covering a mole that now seemed too intimate. "What's the matter, Kat?" J.D. taunted softly. "You seem nervous. You can't take it, can you?" he murmured, running a hand through his hair. "Someone getting too close. What you need is—what do you need, Kat?" he asked, scanning her suddenly pale face.

Katherine had to get away; she could feel the panic rising, her control slipping. In another moment she'd be lashing out at him. "J.D., why don't you cut the examination and find a way out of here?"

He lifted one of those straight, heavy, black eyebrows. "Why, Angel? I haven't even started to examine you," he said, tossing the words at her, watching the color seep up her cheeks.

She hated the telltale flush, the warmth flowing up her throat to her face. "If you don't do something...now, I will."

"Oh? Be my guest, Houdini. When Irish painted the window, she let it dry shut. Short of breaking it, you can forget that way out." J.D. unbuttoned his shirt, and the lamplight glistened in the matted hairs on his chest. He yawned and closed his eyes. "It's been a long day. Travis has a way of running until he falls asleep. Let me know when you've found the escape hatch."

Katherine chewed on her lip, willing him to disappear. He stretched leisurely, opening one eye. "You look like you're about to blow into bits, Kat."

He patted the coverlet. "From the shadows under your eyes I'd say you've missed a few night's sleep. Why don't you come lie down and rest until Irish—?"

"Share a bed with you? When hell freezes over." Katherine frantically started searching the room for something to pick at the lock. Finding nothing, she ran her fingers through her hair to find a tortoiseshell hairpin. Drawing one out, she stared at it for a moment.

Watching her through his lashes, J.D. decided there was really nothing like watching Katherine squirm. In fact, just to watch her do anything was an experience. Her hair tumbled, floating silkily about her bare shoulders. Katherine frowned as she studied the hairpin, forging her plot.

It stunned him then—the thought that Katherine still intrigued him, still made him ache.

He could feel his muscles shift, bunching for a fight. Why hadn't he ever needed another woman the way he'd needed her?

For a second he allowed himself the vision of Katherine moving toward him, sliding into his arms. All silvery hair and black lace, with skin like satin.... J.D. frowned, feeling his tension. Okay, maybe he needed her. Just maybe.

At least long enough to get her out of his system.

Looking pale and fragile, Katherine reached straight into his heart. It was an old weakness, one that apparently still haunted him.

He needed to fold her against him, to protect her from her ghosts, to share *her* needs. He forced himself to swallow, though his throat was dry. He'd always felt that way about Katherine.

She'd slice him into shreds for his weakness....

Katherine took a deep breath, as if preparing for the great escape, and J.D. found himself starting to heat. If ever he wanted to place his hands over a woman's soft breast, it was now.

The gesture would declare his right of possession, obliterating her husband's touch.

The beguiling mauve tips moved within the fragile lace, and J.D. folded his hands across his taut stomach. The lamplight spilled down her silhouette, outlining her shape, from shoulders down to narrow waist, slightly curved hips and long legs.

When she walked purposefully toward the door, he admired the neat sway of those hips. The madame's costume had ridden up, and Katherine's pale buttocks curved gently below. Beads of perspiration began to form on his forehead, while his throat was quietly closing.

Placing the hairpin within the old lock, and turning it, Katherine listened intently. Frustrated, she rattled the brass knob. After a moment she cursed softly, then knelt to peer into the lock. The costume slipped higher and J.D. was unable to look away.

Wanting to strip off the lace and satin, peeling it from his Kat as if to take away the years, J.D. frowned. But if she knew he couldn't control his desire for her—couldn't kill it—she'd love it.

When Katherine sighed and stood up, the madame's chemise had slipped low on her left breast. The view enchanted him. J.D. ached, remembering her soft sighs of pleasure against his mouth.

Had she sighed, sweetly accepting Big Jim?

The pain knifed through him, leaving him chilled.

He could almost feel her softness within his palm, the pebbly texture of her breast as his tongue laved moisture across it—

Katherine slashed a glance at him. Apparently satisfied that he was sleeping, she started looking about the room for another tool. She bent, studying the contents of a small box, and the chemise fell away altogether, exposing the creamy softness of her breasts.

J.D. groaned, longing to bind her to himself. Frustration wrapped around him like a hot glove, tightening his flesh with sensual need. She'd innocently aroused him and he'd let her do it. "Katherine, get the hell off the floor and get into bed!" he snapped, turning away from her.

"You weren't sleeping," she accused him. "Stop telling me what to do."

"Of course not. What man could sleep with a woman dressed like that parading all over the room?"

"Think of me as someone who wishes we'd never met."

He turned slowly toward her and the old bed creaked. Golden sparks flew from her hair as she stood near the bed. "That's pretty impossible, since you're dressed like that."

Reaching out, J.D. slid his palm over her smooth thigh to snap her garter. He chuckled, sensing that Katherine had forgotten how to play. Feeling the warmth, he grinned. She looked as though she'd like to tear him apart. That could be interesting—to have their battles out. "Take it easy, Kat. You're getting all worked up over nothing."

Pushing her hands through her hair, Katherine tossed her head. Now the strands were touched with a silver halo. She shuddered, glancing into the night. "Nothing, he says."

The back of one hand slashed across her eyes. And when it left, her cheeks glistened with tears.

The sight caught J.D. in the midsection with the force of a fighter's punch. He hadn't expected Katherine to cry.

Fighting the emotion, her bottom lip trembling, she glanced uneasily at him, unable to hide the fear dancing beneath her lashes.

Something within J.D. went haywire, softening, warming. He saw her swallow, the pulse beating heavily at the base of her throat, her bones seeming sharp beneath the taut skin.

"I want out of here. Now," she stated huskily, rubbing her hands up and down her arms as though she were freezing.

The uneven, fearful tone of her voice went through J.D. and the need to hold her grew too great. Without thinking he rolled to his feet. Facing her, J.D. placed his hands along her cheeks. Running his thumbs along her damp cheekbones, he frowned. "Kat, calm down. What are you afraid of? Irish will be back soon."

Catching her bottom lip between her teeth, Katherine rested her hands on his wrists. "This is just a game to you, isn't it, J.D.?"

He tested the softness of her lips with his thumbs, gently smoothing the pale flesh beside them—and to his surprise found himself answering truthfully. "No, it's not a game. It's the bottom line."

Her eyes widened and seemed to swallow him, her pupils mirroring his face. She trembled, pressing her fingertips on his wrists. "Leave Irish alone, J.D.," she whispered as though the words were torn from her. "She's not up to your style."

When she breathed, her breasts brushed his lower chest. The musky fragrance from her bath swirled about him, enticing him. "No. But you are, aren't you, sweet Katherine?" he asked slowly, tracing her face, remembering it heated with passion.

"I'm not a girl any longer," she whispered, looking at his mouth. Just that flicker of curiosity sent him on edge. "I'm not looking for some cowboy with too-tight pants, marking stars in his little black book."

Now he caught her uncertainty as her gaze drifted to his hair. "We're not the same people, Kat. And it's too late for what happened in the past. Put your fingers in my hair, Kat. Like you used to. Slide it through your fingers," he urged, knowing that he wanted the touch of her hands.

Gently clawing the hair that covered his wrists, she pressed her fingertips into him. "No."

"Touch me, then," he whispered huskily, feeling tension race through her, breathing the fresh fragrance of her hair. Pressing his mouth against her temple, he rubbed the cool, smooth flesh. "You're still in me, Kat. And I'm still in you," he affirmed, trailing his lips across her damp lashes.

In some sane portion of his brain caution raised its head; yet with Katherine soft and sweet in his arms he didn't care.

She inhaled sharply, shivering as he drew her nearer. "Let me warm you."

Her body stiffened as he kissed a fresh trail across her lids. Laying his cheek against hers, he slid an arm around her waist, his palm slowly caressing the narrow sweep of her back.

Closing his eyes, J.D. savored the taut stance, the unrelenting pride that ruled her. By being gallant he'd hurt her, and now he ached to change the direction of the tide. *She felt so right.*

Gradually her tense muscles eased, her breath sweeping unevenly across his cheek. Testing his own emotions, he breathed lightly, knowing the danger of this smoky-eyed woman. J.D. pressed his lips against her hair, tasting the silky strands as they clung to his mouth. Her hands, trapped between their bodies, rested on his chest, moving slowly, restlessly.

Lifting her face to him, Katherine leaned back slightly. "This isn't right, J.D. You know it isn't. We've hated each other for years. I can't trust you."

Kissing her forehead, he urged, "Then trust yourself. Listen to what you need."

She'd found the stone and was holding it tightly. The thong tightened about his neck, and J.D. allowed himself to be drawn down to her lips.

Suddenly her fingers were in his hair and her mouth was moving sweetly beneath his, beckoning. J.D. succumbed, allowing her lips to trail across his in a soft exploration.

J.D. forced himself not to deepen the kiss. *She had to understand. He'd sent her away for her own good.*

Stark and hot, desire ripped through him, the kind that wanted to throw her onto the bed, strip her and forget the past. But the pleasure would be momentary and he wanted more from Katherine. Placing his hands along her jaw, he carefully raised his head to look at her.

Head back, eyes half-closed, she was gazing at him with a dazed expression. Then panic raced across the wild, gray eyes. It wasn't desire; something else was scurrying in the golden flecks. She began to tremble and her legs folded beneath her.

Sweeping her against him, J.D. felt her arms lock around his neck. At this moment Katherine was using him for a lifeline.

She began to cry softly, quietly trying to control the emotion that was gripping her.

J.D.'s heart stopped with the fragility of the moment. *She'd been his to care for all along.*

Why did he have to touch her as though he cared? Katherine wondered, feeling his hands smooth her hair. J.D. whispered softly against her cheek, kissing her as he would a child. She couldn't trust him; she knew she couldn't. Hadn't she enough scars from him?

God, how could she be so weak, so willing to be swept under his control?

How could she possibly let him within two feet of her?

Why was he so gentle, so tender now?

She couldn't trust J.D. any more than she could a habitual bail jumper.

Katherine placed her palms against his flat stomach and pushed. The thrust sent him off balance and falling backward onto the bed. It creaked once, then the mattress collapsed to the floor in a mound of ruffles, satin robe and sprawling male. The four posts and headboard framed J.D.'s lean body like a miniature fort. "J.D., if I ever want something from you again, I'll ask. Meanwhile don't hold your breath."

Sweeping the back of her hand across her lips, Katherine glared at him. His expression had changed from surprise to anger, the kind that sent a dark rose flush up his cheeks. Rising off the bed, J.D. jerked her to him. The impact of his hard body sent the breath from her.

"Changing horses—or should I say men—in the middle of the stream is just your style, Kat. I could make you crawl...and maybe I will."

She tossed back her hair. "I don't think you can, J.D."

"Really?" he asked, too coolly. "Who are you trying to convince—me or yourself?"

The key sounded in the lock, the door creaked as it swung open, and Irish appeared. "I intended to get this lock fixed—oh, I see you two have been at it again," she intoned, at once sensing the tension in the room. She glanced from Katherine's costume to J.D.'s open shirt, then at their set, angry faces.

"You have a lot to explain. Do you have any more surprises up your sleeve, sister dear?" Katherine asked through clenched teeth.

Travis, his eyes wide, peeked around Irish's thigh, holding her hand. "We heard a big noise."

Flashing a glance about the room, Irish spotted the fallen bed. Slowly she looked back at J.D. and Katherine.

To Katherine's chagrin, J.D. quickly bent to kiss the side of her neck. "We've been wrestling, Travis."

Travis blinked once, then grinned.

Meanwhile Irish was intently studying her sister's hot, furious expression.

"It isn't what you think, Irish," Katherine said, her jaw rigid with anger.

To add to the scenario, J.D. bent and retrieved her robe. Holding it for her, he winked at Irish, then said, "Here, Angel. You'll catch cold."

She jammed her arms through the sleeves, tied the sash and rounded on him. "You're going to catch something else, J.D.," she warned.

"Mmm. I'm waiting. Really I am," he returned lightly.

Irish sighed and shook her head. "Well, it isn't much of an improvement, but at least you two haven't killed each other yet. Come on, Travis. Let's go down and have some nice ice cream, while these two cool off . . . er, fix the bed," she amended.

When Katherine edged by him, J.D.'s hand wrapped itself about her upper arm, staying her. "Let me go, J.D.," Katherine ordered quietly.

"Grandpa?" Travis questioned, a note of uncertainty in his voice.

Flicking a glance at his grandson, J.D. breathed heavily, then stepped back from Katherine, freeing her. He ran an unsteady hand through his hair.

She experienced a sharp pang of pleasure—J.D. was as affected as herself.

"We're fine, son. Go along with Irish."

When Katherine glared at him, J.D. winked, then crouched to repair the bed. "There's no more excitement happening tonight, is there, Angel?"

He'd deliberately taken a shot at her, rolling the name across his lips to remind her that in his opinion she'd sold herself, she decided. Then, she wanted to damage him, experience just a tiny shot of good, clean revenge. Then laugh. She hadn't laughed for eons, and now she knew that if she could give J.D.'s flat backside just one swift kick...

As though sensing her thoughts, J.D. looked over his shoulder. "I wouldn't, if I were you," he said quietly, his dark eyes sparkling with humor.

At two o'clock in the morning Katherine leaned against her window to look down upon the cottage. Outlined in the moonlight and partially veiled by the pines, J.D.'s house held a mystery she couldn't solve.

Sheathed in a silk wrapper, Katherine listened to the coyotes howling. An owl swooped across the silvery disk of the moon. Then she saw J.D. move from the shadows and look up.

Shielded by the lacy curtain, Katherine knew he couldn't see her. Tension swirled about her like a hot, thin wire.

J.D. One man alone, standing lean and menacing, his hard face turned toward her.

Tasting again the sweet flavor of his mouth as it moved softly against hers, Katherine shivered. She could fight his arrogance. Could she fight his tenderness?

Feeling like a runner out of breath, Katherine placed her hand over her heart and moved away.

Five

The next day J.D. sat in a rocker on the inn's back porch, his boots propped on the railing. Katherine slept in a shaded hammock as though she was totally innocent of stirring him up. He scowled at her, then lifted an old daily paper to reread an article titled "Angel Slugs Bogus Car Ring."

According to the newspaper Katherine had been in top form, slashing into a crime ring that turned back odometers. The victims were typically the very young and the very old, Katherine's favorite causes.

J.D. reluctantly admitted his admiration of her ability to rescue the needy. Carefully reading the column, he learned that Katherine had tried to kill the story and minimize her part in the investigation. In fact she'd taken the reporter to task for "blowing out of proportion actions that any attorney would have taken." Then she had informed the reporter that the emphasis of the story should be on means to detect phony car sales, not spotlighting her.

She kept her private life from the media and refused to give interviews, unless it served to alert the public about possible scams.

He tossed the paper aside, feeling edgy. Damn it, he liked the way she handled herself and her profession. She'd shown compassion when it was needed. He pushed the thought away and scowled at her again. So far as he was concerned, she had an overdue payment that he intended to collect.

"I want to talk to you about Travis." J.D. nudged Katherine's bare foot with the tip of his boot. Just drifting into her afternoon nap in the shaded hammock, Katherine refused to open her eyes. She'd had a restless night and a futile morning of trying to approach Irish about J.D.

"Not now." It was her shade tree and her sweet, Colorado breeze. She resented his after-shave infringing on her privacy.

She resented J.D.'s very presence in her life and the way his kiss had stirred her senses. She hadn't wanted to start questioning her sensuality with Big Jim, contrasting the friendly lovemaking they had enjoyed to the almost savage hunger she had barely contained with J.D. When she was more in control, more rested, she was going to kick J.D.'s well-shaped backside with some legality or other.

She allowed one eye to open fractionally, then closed it again. Right now she wanted his shadow off her body.

"Now." When he nudged her toe again, Katherine felt herself begin to gear up for a confrontation.

It was silly, but she considered her toes intimately hers. Without hose and business pumps they seemed too vulnerable, too fragile. The slender extensions were quite special to her, a frivolous bit of femininity to be pampered and pedicured. They loved to curl over lush carpeting or warm, soft grass. It was something she'd kept to herself throughout carving a successful career and running a business empire.

She moved them carefully inside the hammock, away from his damned boot. He'd made her angry again, she realized moodily, hating to retreat. Her heartbeat began to accelerate like a hot rod waiting for a green light.

How was it possible that Katherine Dalton Kelly could burrow even deeper under his skin? J.D. wondered darkly. With her hair loose and catching the dappled sunlight, the breeze playing in the silver and gold lights, she looked—

He jammed his flattened hands into his pockets, watching her and resenting every dram of the attraction that apparently hadn't been dimmed by the years. A butterfly hovered next to her cheek, and Katherine raised a hand to brush it lazily away. The movement arched her slender body, flowing upward from the long legs to the thrust of her breasts.

He could still almost feel that slender-soft body easing onto his last night, feel the give-and-take that was his young, sweet Katherine. When she'd cried softly in his arms, she'd washed away the lonesome years.

Because she'd caused him a long night, remembering how no other woman could ever cut into him, making him ache the way she had, J.D. did what he knew best when it came to approaching Katherine now.

"Okay, Angel," he drawled, watching the flicker of her lids. He intended the cynical tone; she'd sold herself, hadn't she? "Tempting as you may be, I do need to talk to you about Travis."

He rocked the hammock with his boot, enjoying the way Katherine's full lips firmed in anger. A softness rippled beneath her T-shirt, and he found his mouth drying at the thought of her breasts nestled against him. Her long, pale toes curled into the netting, and he suddenly wanted to run his fingertips across them.

He shoved the thought down, along with the memories and the irritation at himself. He didn't want that warm-honey feeling flowing through him. Discovering it, Katherine would slash into the weakness like a trained fencer.

"You know, if you want me to join you, I suppose we could find some way to pass the time of day."

Her eyes shot open and their smoky-gray color burned up at him. "Back off."

He laughed outright. "You may be tired and edgy, but you're fiery as hell around me. Have you ever wondered why?"

That drew her coiling lithely to her feet, her fingers curling slowly into fists. Placing her bare feet apart, Katherine faced him like a fighter squaring off for the last round. Her toes locked into the grass, the hot-pink tips blazing in a patch of sunlight. "Fine. We'll talk about Travis first, then Irish."

Katherine's cheeks were flushed from her brief nap, her eyes snapping at him. He wondered then how it would feel waking up to her after making love. A sudden pain went ricocheting through him. He remembered only too well the soft nestling of her body against his, before reality came to call, all those years ago.

He wanted her to feel some of that pain, too. Drawing a line down her hot cheek, J.D. watched her dance back from the light touch. "You're strung too tight, Kat," he said softly. His tone lacked the taunting edge he'd intended.

He could feel her anger ripple. She wanted to lash out at him. He could deal with her temper; he couldn't deal with the softness he had just started recognizing. "Hell, yes," she snapped. "I'm angry, and you damn well know it."

"Last night was good for me. Was it for you, Angel?" he asked slowly, knowing that her mouth was something he just had to taste. Washed by shade and sunlight, the full contours would be moist and warm. He knew, too, that his taunt would take her over the edge.

As he expected, her hand came jabbing upward and he caught her wrist in his.

This was what he wanted, the white-hot jolt of emotions twisted by the years, fermenting from love into hatred, matching his own. He could meet her on this level, strip her, wound her as she had knifed into him.

Feeling the delicate bones within his grasp, J.D. looked into her furious face. She held herself rigid, refusing to yield to his strength, her head thrown back.

The breeze went riffling through the golden strands of her hair.

God, she was beautiful—mad as hell and anxious to hurt.

Her scent swirled about him, a deep, sensual touch of musk and woman. His fingers moved over the sensitive veins of her inner wrist, testing both the silky-smooth skin and the heat of the passion beating through her.

"How would you like a nice, streamlined harassment suit slapped on you?" she asked tightly. "I'm not fond of getting mauled by someone who outweighs me by about a hundred pounds."

Pleased that he was getting to her, J.D. stepped closer. "All this attention is overwhelming. You're fighting too hard, Kat. It leads a man to think that maybe—"

"Don't think, J.D. You get in trouble when you use your brain."

He smiled at that, conceding against his will that with her silvery eyes flashing at him and her blood pounding beneath his fingertips, Katherine Dalton Kelly was still more woman than any of the others who had occasionally strolled through his life. "If it's harassment you want, I know how to give it to you. But it's Travis that I'm concerned about."

He saw her gray eyes flicker, then shift away from his to locate a stand of aspen trees. Fluttering in the afternoon breeze, the leaves reminded J.D. of the fragile nature of his relationship with Katherine.

"Let go of my arm," she ordered evenly. "I can't stand your touch."

The softly spoken words were like a punch in the stomach, and J.D. swallowed the pain.

"What about Travis?" she asked as he unwillingly moved his fingers. J.D. placed his hand flat on his hard thigh, trying to forget the feel of her skin heating beneath his touch.

"My grandson has fallen beneath your spell," he began, then realized that perhaps both MacLean males had the same problem. He found himself grinding his teeth, tightening the muscles in his jaw at the thought. "He's beginning to transfer his feelings for his mother to you. Last night all he talked about was how you're blond like Daisy."

J.D. felt his eyes flickering involuntarily over the sunlit mass of her hair. To keep his fingers from plunging into the silky warmth, he jammed his palms into his back pockets. "That and the fact that you loved his mother when she was a child. He's susceptible right now to any attachment to his mother, especially from a blonde who keeps giving him hugs. I'm asking you to keep your distance," he stated slowly, watching the drift of sadness come and go in her face.

Katherine's fingers sought the place on her wrist that he had touched, rubbing it as she spoke quietly. "I've been concerned about the same thing myself, J.D. I know the pitfalls of losing someone you love and how it hurts."

The reference to her dead husband sent a wave of nausea through his stomach. Had it been a widow's mourning that sent her into his arms, the warm tears sliding against his throat? "I'm sure you've been well repaid for your grief, Angel," he stated curtly.

She swung her head around, facing him squarely, and the motion fanned her hair into the sweet, summer air before it drifted about her shoulders. J.D.'s fingers curled again; he wanted to grasp the silky strands and draw her mouth to his.

"Travis is a little boy, J.D. He's not all tough and macho like you are—yet. Give him a chance to be loved, will you? Or are you already making decisions for his life, too? You can't always cut the cards the way you want them, you know. Travis is sweet. A part of my Daisy..." Her words escaped into the air; it was as though she'd suddenly revealed a part of herself to him—a part she hadn't intended him to get near.

Suddenly wrapping her arms around herself as if she felt cold, Katherine looked at the ground between them. "I loved Daisy," she murmured simply. "In many ways Travis is like her. I'm aware of the danger of transference, but this time you're asking a lot, J.D.," she continued in an uneven tone.

A single tear slid down her smooth cheek, and J.D. found his throat drying.

She wiped angrily at the damp trail. "I hate this."

He didn't want to feel anything for her but contempt; she needed to pay for his pain. He didn't want to draw her into his arms and gently place her head on his shoulder.

But nothing in heaven or hell could have kept him from doing just that.

Again she cried softly and the sound tore at his heart. He drew her closer, offering her the shelter of his body against the emotion she tried desperately to control but could not.

Stroking his hand down her back, J.D. closed his eyes and savored being snared by the scent and the feel of his Kat. Her hair drifted along his cheek. Catching in the rough texture, it wound itself around the strength of his throat and he felt himself grow weak.

"Oh, J.D.," she whispered raggedly. "I'm so tired."

Running his hand beneath her hair, he stroked the taut muscles, knowing that he couldn't step away. She trembled, still fighting for control, and slipped back into quiet tears as he held her. "I miss her," she whispered helplessly. "Oh, God, I can't stop crying—last night and today. Do something."

"I can't," he admitted rawly after a moment, surprised and thrown off balance by the sudden discovery. J.D. couldn't think of a time he'd cried since reaching manhood. Now Katherine brought his emotions writhing to the surface, casually destroying his scorn as if it were no more than dandelion fluff before a stormy wind. Placing his cheek beside hers, he rubbed its moisture gently against her damp skin. They were both wrapped up in the memories, both aching and hurting, warriors of the years, scarred and tough, yet each needing the other.

"Oh, God...Oh, God," she repeated, wrapping her arms around his waist and holding on.

As the lazy, afternoon shadows enfolded them, J.D. urged her against the wall of a small shed. Still shielding her with his body, he rode the wild emotions that were breaking loose in each of them.

"I can't stand this . . . weakness," she uttered, her husky tone pulling his mouth lower to kiss away her pain. He knew what it cost her to reveal any portion of herself to him, so the simple fact that she'd lost control and had asked him to help her sent him reeling.

She was his sweet Kat again, needing him.

Once his lips touched her moist, warm ones, J.D. forgot about everything but wanting to drown himself and the empty years in Katherine's willing offering.

She raised her face and her mouth accepted the light brush of his across her cheeks. Her lips found his, tasted and retreated shyly.

Moving her deeper into his embrace, J.D. breathed lightly as her scent hovered around him. "Come here."

There in the shadows the years fell away as she lifted her arms and locked them around his neck.

J.D.'s hands glided slowly down her body, tracing the sweet curves instinctively. She raised her mouth, parted her lips and accepted the gentle foray of his tongue. She moved into him and J.D. found himself melting.

The kisses were brief, offering just a taste of pleasure in the rediscovery of the excitement that was racing between them.

He felt himself skimming across sensual depths, bathing in the feel of her near him.

His Kat. His woman.

She was purring now, stroking her slender hand across his chest, finding both the talisman and his heart. The feminine sound deep in her throat urged him to intensify the kiss.

Her hands moved restlessly across the hair covering his chest, exploring it. They were shaking with passion as Katherine tried to satisfy a hunger that had not dimmed.

J.D.'s hands wandered through the layers of denim and cotton, sought and found the softness he wanted. He heard her catch her breath as he found her breasts, cupping them, running his thumbs across the hardened tips.

Then she moved closer, drawing them both deeper into the fire.

Placing his hands beneath her hips, molding the softness with his palms, J.D. gently lifted her against him. He watched her face, saw hot excitement racing beneath the smooth skin. He felt her soft thighs ease against his hard ones and lifted her higher. He felt her tremble as she clung to him, and the absolutely feminine gesture devastated J.D. as nothing by any other woman ever had.

Katherine had been his lover once, and he needed her again to make him whole.

Her scents captivated, destroyed—and kept him coming back for more. Her lips tugged at his hard mouth, making him weak. Her hands pushed him back, then tugged him closer, the sounds coming from her protesting, yet needing.

Irish's call seemed so distant, so unimportant. He resented the intrusion, wanting the flame in his Kat to burn away the pain he still felt.

Irish called again, and Katherine grew still, trembling in his arms, her hot face buried against his throat. He could feel her tense as she withdrew from him, and the pain came raging back.

Then she struggled and he held her still, watching her with furious eyes.

She met his fury and returned it with her own. In the seconds that passed each battled silently for control.

Katherine knew how to reach inside and score a hit, he decided as she composed her features. The tears were still damp on her cheeks, yet she refused to let him see her wipe them away.

"Can you control this, Angel, like you control everything else?" he asked, a shade too carefully, moving his hands to press her harshly against him.

Through the tension they heard a childish voice. "Grandpa...Kat! My mama guppy is having babies! Come see 'em!"

J.D. allowed Kat to slide slowly down his aroused body, wanting her to feel the need she'd aroused.

"Shall we?" Stepping clear of his reach the moment she was free, Katherine coolly lifted her eyebrows. J.D. felt the raw nerves stretch tightly within him. A moment ago she'd been as much affected as he.

Following the neat sway of her backside and down the long length of those legs encased in the tight, worn jeans, J.D. had the feeling that he was traveling on a dangerous, switchback road at night—with no brakes.

Throughout the early evening the fifteen baby guppies slipped one by one from their mother. Aided by Katherine and Irish, Travis scooped them into a net and deposited them in a smaller tank for safety. Between numbers eight and nine, Irish insisted that everyone eat bagels stuffed with alfalfa sprouts and tuna salad. They had just toasted baby number nine with glasses of milk when number ten arrived.

Standing aside, J.D. found himself watching Katherine with an intensity he didn't want. In the excitement, her delighted squeals as the guppies emerged caught him broadside.

Katherine bent to view the babies in the small aquarium, and her T-shirt rode up, revealing the smooth expanse of her back. J.D. remembered the dip and slender curve beneath the span of his hand....

J.D. rubbed his palm across his jaw uneasily. She had him tripping back in time; it was too dangerous.

She'd been just as thrilled as he had when Daisy took her first step. With her face shining and scrubbed, her hair back in a ponytail, Katherine had grinned at him. On the floor, holding Daisy close, she looked more child than young woman, and he'd suddenly felt very old. "We've got a surprise, Dad. Daisy took her first step today."

He'd answered something appropriate, knowing that she was too young for him. He knew, too, even back then, that without her the years would be lonely. She had gotten slowly to her feet, frowning. Her hand had smoothed his hair from his forehead, her gray eyes concerned. "Bad day, J.D.?"

His truck had broken down with a fresh load of produce, and a bill collector had turned up, demanding cash payment. He'd wanted to hold her then, to wrap himself in the sweet softness she silently offered.

But even then people were saying that Katherine had a great future waiting for her. He couldn't ask her to trade that for bills and hardship.

Now he found himself wondering what the years would have been like with her instead of the dreams.

Holding Travis's hand, Katherine bent her head toward the lighted tank, tracing the mother's pathway. "Here comes . . . number twelve! Travis, are you ready?"

Travis grinned widely, then concentrated on the task of scooping up the tiny fish. "Yup. Got him!"

"Travis, the great guppy hunter!" Katherine exclaimed, hugging him to her. "Hey, here comes number thirteen. Hurry up."

J.D. absently noted Irish's curious glances, then lost himself hopelessly in the magic of Katherine.

Irish slipped out the door unnoticed as number fourteen came scooting free, and Katherine swung around unexpectedly to meet J.D.'s eyes. The hunger and loneliness that burned in them anchored her to the spot.

"Now you've done it," he said ominously, then moved to help Travis collect the fifteenth guppy.

The promising, yet savage look had shaken her, terrifying her more than any court trial she had experienced. She rubbed her trembling hands against her thighs, trying to push back the emotions that were rocking her.

She had cried in his arms and he had comforted her tenderly.

They had kissed; a mutual, sweet tasting and then the savage need...

She recognized his expression; J.D. was on a course set straight for her, and they both knew it would end in collision—and disaster.

"Kat?" Travis's small hand tugged at hers.

"Mmm?" Katherine crouched beside the boy, running her hand affectionately through his black hair. Travis had snared her heart, and with J.D.'s permission or not, she wanted to be with the boy.

His dark eyes watched her drowsily, his hand holding hers tightly. "Don't go 'way. Hold me."

So much fear for one so young, she thought as she sat down in a rocker and Travis climbed onto her lap. Watching her solemnly, he kissed her cheek, smoothing the area with his hand. "Nice."

When she kissed him back, she heard J.D. clear his throat and move restlessly from the shadows.

Looming over her, he drew his brows together; a strand of hair fell across his forehead. He looked like what he was—tough, untamed and deeply irritated. Anger crackled about him like lightning in a Rocky Mountain storm, a muscle in his jaw convulsing with increasing tempo. "Be careful, Kat," he warned softly.

Katherine drew Travis more comfortably against her, needing the protection of the boy against J.D. She knew what he was thinking. He didn't want her too close to any part of him; *he* wanted to call the shots.

Why had he cried earlier? Wondering that, she took in the rugged features, the rough stubble beginning to darken his jaw. "I'm so sorry about Daisy," she repeated softly.

J.D. looked away uneasily, his profile sharp in the dimly lighted room. "Travis is here," he said in a gravelly voice that she suspected covered deep emotion. "He's mine now."

Travis wrapped his hand in Katherine's hair and snuggled to her breast. Watching J.D.'s harsh expression as he turned, Katherine deliberately wrapped her arms around the little boy. Over Travis's head she returned the look evenly. If J.D. wanted to play the role of heavy-handed, possessive grandfather now, he'd have to fight her.

Holding Travis against her, she began to rock slowly. She needed the boy's warmth to fight the cold memories. But more than that, Travis needed the security of her arms; she'd give him that for a time, and J.D. could simmer until the sky dropped. The creak of the old rocker heightened the tension in the room as memories swirled between them.

Travis's fingers moved in her hair, stroking it. "Grandpa, play for me," he murmured sleepily.

J.D.'s expression darkened savagely; he reached down to stroke Travis's hair. The gesture brought his fingertips coursing lightly across Katherine's upper breast and she stopped breathing, her throat dry. J.D. jerked back his hand as though burned. "When you're in bed, sport. Kat wants to go home."

When Travis started, his eyes round and questioning, Katherine drew his head back to her shoulder. She gathered him tighter, leaned her head against the rocker and murmured quietly, "I do? I've got time, if Travis wants me a little longer."

"Grandpa?" Travis's plea was even sleepier this time.

Katherine saw uncertainty come and go in J.D.'s hard expression. When he began to shake his head, Katherine began to rock slowly. "Be a fire-breathing dragon some other time, J.D. Play for us."

J.D.'s eyes glittered beneath the shadows of his lashes. He slid his fingers into the soft mass of her hair, crushing it. "You're playing with fire, Angel...but whatever you say."

"Sing, too, Grandpa," Travis urged, turning to look at J.D. He reached to wrap J.D.'s thumb in childish fingers. The two MacLean males exchanged a quiet look, then J.D. nodded slowly.

"So I'm a pushover for a kid with guppies. Two songs, then you hit the hay, okay?"

The songs were country ballads, done in the raw, smoky style that was J.D.'s alone. His hands moved slowly across the strings of the worn guitar. The music was soothing. Katherine closed her eyes, listening to the deep, sensual voice. Years ago it had drawn customers to the bars J.D. had worked when he was done with his trucking runs. Back then he'd needed the extra money, and had practiced for Daisy and Kat in odd moments.

Closing her eyes and rocking the sleeping boy, Katherine felt her taut nerves begin to loosen. Resting her chin on Travis's head, she allowed the soft chords to flow through her, drawing her back to the almost reverent kisses of the afternoon, the sweet gentleness of his arms when she'd cried.

When had the music stopped and the peace begun? she wondered drowsily, feeling someone lift Travis from her.

All the sleepless nights and long days wrapped themselves around her, anchoring her to the chair as her eyes drifted shut. She protested only mildly when the gentle hands lifted her, too.

A clock chimed in the distance and Katherine sleepily counted two bells. Enclosed so safely in her nest, she didn't want to wake up.

She ran her hand across the sheet that covered her, and her palm skimmed a rough patch of warm hair.

The pillow beneath her head was hard, and a man's scent swirled about her as she slowly opened her eyes. The crisp hair covering his chest tickled her nose, and she wiggled it slightly.

J.D. slept, his face tucked in her hair. His arm tightened about her, drawing her closer. He nuzzled her hair and uttered a low growl of contentment as his broad palm slid slowly upward to cup her breast. His long fingers kneaded the softness, and the growl deepened sensually.

Katherine swallowed, feeling her back nudged by a small knee. Travis sighed in his sleep and edged another knee into her spine. Trapped by the two MacLean males, one tugging at her heartstrings and the other becoming firmly aroused as he shifted his bare thigh against her, Katherine swallowed again. Though J.D. had left her dressed, only a sheet covered them as they lay over the blankets.

Beneath that sheet, J.D. wore briefs that did nothing to disguise that arousal.

"J.D.," she whispered urgently as his mouth glided along her cheek. "Wake up!" She gritted her teeth against the hot sensuality she felt flowing between them. He'd probably had plenty of experience waking up to lovemaking, but she did not.

Her time with Big Jim flashed into her mind. Their subdued lovemaking had always been arranged for the early-evening hours. A shaft of guilt cut through her, and she tugged impatiently at J.D.'s wrist.

When the thumb didn't stop its caressing, Katherine jerked a whorl of the hair on his chest.

"Mmm?" Slowly one lid rose, and beneath the long lashes a black eye peered at her. "What's wrong?"

His toes began to play lazily with her instep, then moved to toy with her toes.

Katherine grew still, surprised by a wave of sensuality. Her toes seemed to flex against his larger ones, arching like kittens to a stroking hand. The thought sent her reeling. "Let me up," she said between her teeth.

Travis's chubby hand plopped onto her cheek and rested there. J.D.'s eyes twinkled as he carefully moved the small hand aside. "Travis has been sleeping with me until he feels safer," he explained. "There was plenty of room for you, too."

His tone sent shivers up Katherine's spine and reminded her of lovers pausing on warm, rumpled sheets. "Let me up," she repeated as his warm foot drifted along the bottom of hers. His toes caught hers and rubbed them.

"Can't." He nuzzled aside her hair to find her ear, nibbling on it. "You'll have to crawl over me. It would be much simpler for everyone if you'd just go back to sleep."

Part of her wanted to turn toward him; she wanted the play of his tongue against her own, the heat igniting between them. "No. Get up."

He reached for the edge of the sheet to draw it back. "If you insist...."

She could feel the shape of the briefs beside her.... She grabbed his wrist and found her fingers quickly laced with his. His thumb caressed the back of her knuckles while she glared at him. "You're being difficult," she accused him in a whisper.

"Count on it," he returned easily, beginning to grin. "I enjoy watching you squirm. But if you don't shut up, you'll wake Travis, and we could be three in bed all night, Goldilocks."

Narrowing her eyes at him, Katherine nudged his trespassing toes away from her own. With a determination she did not feel, she began the slow, perilous task of squirming across J.D.'s body. She paused on top of him, just as a broad palm skimmed her backside and his hips rose suggestively. "You're doing that deliberately. Stop."

"Who, me?" His answering whisper lacked innocence; both hands molded her hips, pressing her slightly into him.

Katherine scooted quickly across him. Standing free, she placed her hands on her waist and glared at him. She didn't want to view the heart-stopping picture the two males created: one so lovable and boyish and the other devastatingly rumpled in shades of sun-kissed skin and dark hair.

With rippling muscles, with hair veering past his navel and the sheet slipping lower.... Her gaze swept down the long, hard, rugged body....

Startled by the immediate cry of the hunger rising in her, Katherine turned and ran for the door, but J.D.'s soft laughter followed her outside.

Alone in her bedroom the next night, Katherine decided that trying to rest with J.D. turning up unexpectedly at any time of night or day was like trying to slide across thin ice on a mountain pond. At any moment her control could break, and she could sink into an unwanted memory that the years should have killed.

Katherine briskly rubbed her hands, watching J.D. and Travis from her darkened bedroom window.

Sprawled on a blanket beneath the stars, J.D. had Travis tucked within the nook of one arm and was pointing to the Colorado night sky. Beside J.D.'s long body, dressed in a T-shirt and jeans, Travis looked like a tiny replica.

Katherine ran a finger across her lips, thinking how gentle J.D. was with his grandson, perfectly attuned to the small boy's needs.

J.D. was an expert at recognizing needs, she thought darkly, remembering the way his mouth had lingered softly over hers.

But he was out for blood. During the day, his every look slashed, cut and accused. He deliberately called her Angel in that slow drawl, reminding her how he thought she'd sold herself. At other times the look held and lingered and warmed, recalling his tender kisses and the firm length of his body as she had crawled across him. If he could get to her, he would.

Irish, on the other hand, thought J.D. was the perfect choice of partner. Watching J.D. carefully ease a sleeping Travis into his arms and carry him into the house, Katherine frowned.

Katherine wrapped her arms around herself and knew two things for certain. Somehow J.D. had the rare ability to make her lose control of her emotions; her response to him was immediate and savage, spiced with a desire she was just beginning to recognize. And while she feared for Irish, her sister was obviously guilty of some still undiscovered crime.

Six

―――

Katherine tapped her fingers against her desk blotter. She'd returned to Denver to keep up the most necessary problems—one of which was regaining her grasp on sanity.

Reviewing those problems, Katherine groaned aloud. Irish was absolutely enthralled with J.D.'s ideas to "awaken the madame." Travis had wrapped himself about Katherine so closely that she dreaded the end of summer. J.D. was encouraging Irish's dreams of plans for a health spa for stressed-out people in business—an activity that Irish considered a dark, but necessary evil. Added to all the previous woes, Irish never stopped giving a sales pitch when it came to J.D.'s good points, such as his donations to charities.

Katherine ran her fingers along the blotter. Putting Irish within talking distance of J.D. was like placing a lighted match next to tinder. They were deeply in cahoots.

Enchanted with J.D.'s idea of incorporating Abagail's legend into a miniplay and roulette party for charity, Irish couldn't be happier.

Giving up all pretense of being interested in Mandy's list of necessaries, Katherine kicked off her shoes, rubbed her feet briskly on the plush carpeting and wondered about the guppies.

She turned to view Denver's skyline and wondered if Irish's new mud bath, a mixture of health clay and various herbal juices, would be successful.

She caught herself thinking about J.D. and Big Jim. While Big Jim had provided an anchor in her life, J.D. made her feel as if she were sitting on nitroglycerin during an earthquake.

Katherine reached out, snared a pencil and snapped it in half. The gesture surprised her. By the end of the summer she intended to have disposed of all the lingering problems with MacLean for all time.

Katherine managed to squeeze in another week at the inn. July 1 was hot and dry. Above the uneven purring of a bulldozer a mockingbird trilled, its early-morning song carrying into the open window of her tiny bedroom. Furnished only with Katherine's computer, desk and chair, the room provided a measure of protection from Irish. Her sister believed that office work belonged in cities and that Katherine needed lots of fresh, country air, so Irish studiously worked at taking Katherine for walks, and monitored her diet and rest like a mother hen.

Katherine leaned closer to the computer screen, taking notes from the legal library service. The words seemed to run together, and her eyes ached behind the fashionable glasses. Discarding them, she leaned back in her chair, allowing the fresh breeze to sweep over her. Rubbing the taut muscles at the back of her neck, she noted that the sounds of excavation had stopped. J.D. could apparently rearrange the mountains as easily as he had installed himself in

Irish's life. Katherine momentarily allowed herself to drift along with the mockingbird's song and the sweet scents of Irish's flower garden.

J.D. and Travis were also regular visitors at the bed-and-breakfast, and somehow J.D. always seemed to be lurking about—"puttering," Irish called it. The current outdoor project was to build a large vegetable and flower garden with an irrigation system feeding from the tiny stream. Irish had convinced J.D. that gardening was therapeutic, a restful exercise for guests.

Irish thrust her head through the window and grinned. "Hey, wanna come out and play? We need a pitcher. Come on, get your nose out of that stuff. I thought you came here to vacation."

"My practice isn't something I can turn my back on, vacation or not," Katherine returned with a smile.

"Ah, the price of success." Irish rested her head on the backs of her hands, studying Katherine. Taking in her sister's T-shirt and jeans, Irish surmised, "I haven't heard you laugh yet. Not once. And you're still clamming up on me. I know something is wrong. And if you think you can hold out all summer against my wily brain, you've got another think coming."

A hand in a worn, leather glove lifted aside the frilly curtain and J.D. appeared, leaning down to peer at her. Atop his grandfather's shoulders, Travis grinned at her, his legs draped across J.D's broad, mud-smeared chest.

Katherine almost winced. Savage that he was, naturally J.D. flaunted his tanned torso with its accompanying rippling muscles and enticing hair.

Her fingers tingled with the urge to rummage through those black, glistening whorls.

Katherine felt sick, confused and very angry—all in a fraction of a second.

J.D. grinned, speaking in a stage whisper to Irish. "She's a stuffed shirt. Can't laugh. Doesn't know how. Let her mold with her computer."

"Hey, Kat—" Travis had picked up her nickname "—come outside. I got a new bat and ball." He wrapped his arms around J.D.'s forehead, and the two, grandfather and grandson, looked at her with the same dark features...the same devil-may-care grin.

"She's afraid," J.D. murmured, watching her intently. "She's stuck in that room like the Hole in the Wall Gang. She's afraid if she comes out we'll nab her. Besides, girls don't make good baseball players, anyway. They're too soft." Katherine could feel the flow of his gaze over her T-shirt and jeans.

For just an instant she felt young again, excitement racing through her like clean, sweet rain falling onto a mountain flower. Katherine could feel a smile tug at the corners of her mouth.

To taunt her, he smiled that slow, seductive, all-male smile. "You're looking pretty this morning, Miss Katherine. Come out and play."

Irish punched his shoulder lightly. "She's got that stubborn snail look again. I vote you toss her in the medicinal mud bath. I need to test the clay mixture."

"Oh, no, you don't!" Katherine turned off her computer and stood.

"Do it, J.D. I dare you," Irish returned relentlessly. "I want her in the mud bath. Now."

"By Jove, I think you've got something," J.D. murmured, setting Travis down. "Are you coming out, Miss Katherine? Or am I coming in after you?" he asked, too pleasantly.

One long finger rose and slowly crooked, motioning to her. "Come here." The gesture was slow, arrogant and male.

Katherine folded her arms; no one shoved her around, much less had her at their beck and call. "I'm working now. Sorry. Maybe some other time."

"Well, then," he said, easing a long leg through the window. Folding himself carefully, he slipped completely

WOW!

THE MOST GENEROUS
FREE OFFER EVER!
From the
Silhouette Reader Service™

GET 4 FREE BOOKS WORTH $10.00

Affix peel-off stickers to reply card

4 FOUR FREE BOOKS **4**

4 FOUR FREE BOOKS **4**

PLUS A FREE VICTORIAN PICTURE FRAME

AND A FREE MYSTERY GIFT!

NO COST! NO OBLIGATION TO BUY!
NO PURCHASE NECESSARY!

Because you're a reader of Silhouette romances, the publishers would like you to accept four brand-new Silhouette Desire® novels, with their compliments. Accepting this offer places you under no obligation to purchase any books, ever!

ACCEPT FOUR BRAND NEW
YOURS

We'd like to send you four free Silhouette novels, worth $10.00, to introduce you to the benefits of the Silhouette Reader Service™. We hope your free books will convince you to subscribe, but that's up to you. Accepting them places you under no obligation to buy anything, but we hope you'll want to continue your membership in the Reader Service.

So unless we hear from you, once a month we'll send you six additional Silhouette Desire® novels to read and enjoy. If you choose to keep them, you'll pay just $2.24* each—a saving of 26¢ off the cover price. And there is *no* charge for delivery. There are *no* hidden extras! You may cancel at any time, for any reason, just by sending us a note or a shipping statement marked "cancel" or by returning any shipment of books to us at our cost. Either way the free books and gifts are yours to keep!

ALSO FREE!
VICTORIAN PICTURE FRAME

This lovely Victorian pewter-finish miniature is perfect for displaying a treasured photograph—and it's yours *absolutely free*—when you accept our no-risk offer.

Perfect for a treasured Photograph

Plus a FREE mystery Gift! follow instructions at right.

*Terms and prices subject to change without notice.
Sales taxes applicable in New York and Iowa.
© 1990 HARLEQUIN ENTERPRISES LIMITED

SILHOUETTE DESIRE® NOVELS
FREE!

Silhouette Reader Service™

```
┌─────────────────────────────┐
│                             │
│         AFFIX               │
│    FOUR FREE BOOKS          │
│      STICKER HERE           │
│                             │
└─────────────────────────────┘
```

YES, send me my four free books and gifts as explained on the opposite page. I have affixed my "free books" sticker above and my two "free gift" stickers below. I understand that accepting these books and gifts places me under no obligation ever to buy any books; I may cancel at anytime, for any reason, and the free books and gifts will be mine to keep!

225 CIS JAZJ (U-SIL-D-09/90)

NAME
_____
(PLEASE PRINT)

ADDRESS _____ APT. _____

CITY _____

STATE _____ ZIP _____

Offer limited to one per household and not valid to current Silhouette Desire® subscribers. All orders subject to approval.

```
┌───────────────────┐   ┌───────────────────┐
│    AFFIX FREE     │   │                   │
│    VICTORIAN      │   │   AFFIX FREE      │
│     PICTURE       │   │  MYSTERY GIFT     │
│      FRAME        │   │  STICKER HERE     │
│   STICKER HERE    │   │                   │
└───────────────────┘   └───────────────────┘
```

PRINTED IN U.S.A.

WE EVEN PROVIDE FREE POSTAGE!

It costs you *nothing* to send for your free books — we've paid the
postage on the attached reply card. And we'll pick up the postage
on your shipment of free books and gifts, and also on any subsequent
shipments of books, should you choose to become a subscriber. Unlike
many book clubs, we charge *nothing* for postage and handling!

BUSINESS REPLY MAIL
FIRST CLASS   PERMIT NO. 717   BUFFALO, NY

POSTAGE WILL BE PAID BY ADDRESSEE

Silhouette Reader Service™

P.O. BOX 1867
BUFFALO, NY 14240-9952

NO POSTAGE
NECESSARY
IF MAILED
IN THE
UNITED STATES

through the opening to stand upright before her. "You leave me no choice."

J.D. stripped off his gloves and tossed them to the floor.

The summer breeze caught the gossamer lace curtain, its rose pattern brushing his shoulders like a lover's caress. Standing in a strip of sunlight, Katherine faced him, her hands on her waist.

The varnished hardwood boards stretched between them like the years, worn, yet with a rich patina that lingered.

J.D. paused for a moment, admiring Katherine's stance. Head held high, having no fear of the devil himself, she challenged his baser instincts. Was this how she stood in court? he wondered.

But over the dark, smoky eyes perched an intriguing, precarious little roll of hair. She'd thrust pencils through the loose knot, and strands had slid down her slender neck. A damp tendril clung to her cheek.

Wisping around her face, the strands begged to be fully released. Like the woman who had sobbed in his arms two weeks ago. She'd hated that—the lapse from her isolation, her safety—and hated him for being the one she'd turned to. Her eyes flashing at him, she'd silently dared him to mention her momentary weakness.

It wasn't easy staying out of Katherine's way. Against his will J.D. found himself waiting for a glimpse of her, waiting for the elusive scent of her musky perfume. When she walked through the fields with Irish, J.D. couldn't help but trace her path.

She'd laugh herself into kingdom come if she knew that once he'd almost killed himself drinking, thinking of her....

J.D. needed a little payback. For all the years. For the last two sleepless weeks, when all he could think of was her hungry mouth, the desperate thrust of her body against his—

The delicate, rosebud wallpaper emphasized her femininity. Katherine glared at him, her legs locked in a fighting stance, her face flushed with anger. Beneath the T-shirt slogan that read Angel Is Always Right, Katherine's small breasts moved freely as she shifted her weight.

A real woman, J.D. thought. One who could send him to hell with a glance—or heaven with a touch.

Allowing himself a smile, J.D. breathed quietly, feeling his heart lurch within his ribs. She'd waltzed around him for years, through the days and through his dreams.

Her eyes flicked across his bare chest. He knew Katherine preferred him in a suit, more comfortable with fighting him that way. J.D. felt the weight of her gaze skitter across his flesh like nervous, silky fingers. He liked that: the shifting of her long legs, the squaring of her shoulders.

"Get out," she ordered in a hushed tone, a silvery strand sliding down the silky nape of her neck. "My office has just sent me word that you've linked your name with mine in Irish's pre-holiday auction. I want that story killed."

He spoke as quietly. "Cool down, Kat. We had to get started on the press in advance. You don't hold a posh event on a moment's notice."

Repeating the columnist's words, she spaced out the words, lashing them at him. "Two of the most eligible singles in Denver, Katherine Kelly and J. D. MacLean, will be romancing each other at Abagail's House. In fact they've both checked into the inn for the summer to start practicing for the event. This reporter has heard rumors that MacLean has dibs on the Avenging Angel for the evening."

Katherine snatched a pencil from her hair and snapped it in two. She threw down the pieces between them. "Don't you ever use my name without my permission. Especially to a magazine that makes its living feeding off gossip."

"The interviewer wanted to know something about Irish. She perked up when I mentioned your name. She's been hanging around Kodiak, asking questions about the two of us. She got an angle on the fact that you and I knew each other years ago—that you babysat for Daisy and I was divorced. I think she even wanted to hear that you and I—"

Her eyes stroked contemptuously down his body. "How like you to slither in on the skirts of a charity function."

Tilting his head, J.D. savored the sight of the imperious, furious woman before him. She hadn't given an inch in years, fighting for her underdogs with a passion that he sensed had still not been fully tapped. Catching a blast of it the other night had tantalized him. He couldn't have left the room if he'd wanted to. "You and I have a date with the mud baths, Miss Katherine," he said, enjoying the way her eyes widened. "If you're worried about your honorable dignity, there's plenty of privacy there with the fence and the willows."

"Pick her up, Grandpa," Travis suggested from the window.

Katherine narrowed her eyes in warning. But J.D. caught the pulse beating rapidly in her throat, the uneven lift and fall of her breasts. "I'd worry about permanent damage if I were you, J.D.," she warned quietly. "We're not kids anymore. I don't fight fair."

"You never did. And I wasn't a kid." He smiled, enjoying the moment, tasting her flavor as it swirled around him. She could make his flesh dance, he remembered, when she dug in her heels. He could almost feel her pulse, the throb of her bones—the excitement of holding Katherine against him. The full, revved-up feeling she gave him, as if life were starting all over again.

A man could wait centuries for a woman like Katherine.

From the window Irish threw in her own incentive. "J.D., so help me, if she doesn't go into the Beauty Bog, you're out a piece of my cherry pie!"

"I'll sue the shorts right off you, J.D.," Katherine stated, lowering her voice. "Manhandling a woman would be just your style—" The words went out of her in a soft whoosh as he bent and swung her over his shoulder.

"You don't know anything about my style, lady. Or you might know that I don't always wear shorts." Straightening, J.D. couldn't resist patting her bottom as she squirmed and hit his backside with her fists. And in the minutes it took him to carry her to the mud bath, he learned that Denver's avenging angel could hold her own with any salty-mouthed seaman.

"Nice mouth, but my parents were married." He grinned, patting her denim-covered hips again. The smooth play of softness shielding muscles felt good, and the curve fitted neatly into his palm. Hauling Katherine around beneath the blue, Colorado sky had made him come alive.

"Hey!" At a sharp pinch to his backside, he took a long-legged skip to avoid more pain. She was no easy case, but no other woman could bring up his senses just by sheer old-fashioned orneriness, J.D. thought as he carefully deposited his squirming burden into the soft goo.

Watching the elegant backside of the owner of the Kelly millions hit the mud, J.D. settled back for the fireworks.

As Katherine landed, the squishy mass oozed about her like warm, sticky chocolate. He saw her lips form a silent "Ooh!" and she lifted her dripping hands to stare at them. While she was stunned, he tossed a word over his shoulder to Irish. "I'd prefer Travis were elsewhere before she catches her breath, okay? We'll play ball another time, and he's learned enough new phrases for one day."

Irish nodded, her grin impish. "Hey, Kat. Make sure you get some on your face. I've been thinking of adding some cucumber and aloe to the base."

Without taking his eyes from Katherine, J.D. spoke quietly to his grandson. "Kat is okay, we're just having fun. She's not going to run away or get mad at you."

"Kat?" The boy's eyes shot to her, then back to his grandfather.

"I'm fine," she said carefully, forcing a smile. "Run before he tosses you in here, too."

A large dollop of blue goo splattered against J.D.'s cheek. The effort threw Katherine forward into the mire, braced on her hands and knees.

Wiping the stuff away with one hand, J.D. began to laugh. He stopped when Irish's forceful shove landed him beside Katherine.

Taking Travis's hand, Irish whispered, "Let's finish off those brownies before those two make us share, huh?"

Struggling to sit up, J.D. heard a sound, a soft giggle that grew. Katherine pelted him with another handful that landed directly on his face. Grinning at him, it was clearly her turn to laugh. "It's good to see you knocked off your high and mighty vine, Tarzan."

J.D. rubbed a hand across his face, wiping away the mud as he listened. There wasn't any sound like it, he decided as Katherine's merriment spread around him like the morning sunlight. It reached inside him, tearing at the darkness, the loneliness.

Years of hating Katherine fell away like dead grass before new, green shoots.

"Come on, Travis, run!" Irish yelled. "Head for the high hills! Don't you guys come in the house until you're hosed off!"

Placing her hand on the nearest support—J.D.'s shoulder—Katherine tried to get to her feet but slipped, landing on top of him.

His arms went around her, taking her weight. For an instant the length of her body melded with his, their legs intertwined.

The smile on the soft mouth that he longed to taste fell still. They'd taste of cinnamon and a dark, sweet earthy essence, he decided, watching her tongue nervously lave moisture across her full bottom lip.

A strand of her sun-warmed hair touched his own lips, tantalizing him with the sweet, musky fragrance of wildflowers.

Sunlight danced through the swaying willow branches, weaving patterns about them as they lay, breathing heavily, staring at each other.

J.D. reached out to draw his fingers across her mud-splattered cheek. The touch was a caress, so light it could have been the July breeze.

Her fingertips moved slightly, testing the hard contour of his shoulder with exquisite care. Beneath her his heart throbbed heavily, as though it waited for the moment to pass. In the distance a cow lowed, calling to her calf. Katherine wanted to move. But she remained braced, her hands at his shoulders.

Muscle and sinew rippled as her fingers dug into them. J.D.'s eyes flickered beneath his lashes, the shadows of the morning easing his hard-boned face. Suddenly the world seemed to shift, the warmth of the sunlight mingling with her tension, wrapping them in a silken web.

She touched him then, following an impulse. Tracing his cheekbones, she savored the roughness that chafed at her fingertips. Then lower, the harsh, male feel of his jaw. She smoothed the square shape of his chin, testing the lines framing his mouth.

Catching the tip of her finger with his teeth, J.D. held her lightly, letting her explore the rugged shape of his face.

The breeze riffled his hair, grown longer now and tapering down his neck. The blue-black strands lifted, taunting her to sift them through her fingers. The sunlight glistened in a streak of silver, its texture enticing her.

They were warm, she thought absently. The two of them, wrapped in goo and sun and something else that bound them together.

J.D. traced the shape of her face with his eyes in a slow, gentle perusal. "I like to hear you laugh," he murmured quietly, so softly that the whispering willows almost buried the tender sound.

He'd caught her broadside, she realized slowly. The deep, intimate tone wrapped itself about her like a lover's spell.

Sliding his hand beneath her T-shirt, he stroked her back, molding the sleek shape with his palm, kneading gently with his strong fingers. Then slowly, so slowly that she barely felt him move, he raised himself to kiss her chin. The kiss was angled, carefully planted on a tiny square of clean skin.

She closed her eyes, willing the brief touch of his lips to linger. When she reopened her eyes, questioning him, J.D. murmured roughly, "You're beautiful."

Reluctantly given, the compliment tingled around her, making her wait for something more. J.D. was breathing unevenly and his fingers were trembling slightly on her flesh. Flickering across her face, his gaze glittered with an excitement she could feel.

No one but J.D. had ever done that.

Without speaking he shifted her gently, rising to his feet. Offering her his hands, he waited.

With the sunlight and the willows and the moment weaving between them, Katherine slipped her hands into his. Lifting her to her feet, J.D. cupped his palms about her shoulders, running his touch across her fine bones to her throat. Resting against her neck, his fingers stopped.

Katherine's heart struggled to beat, awaiting the moment when his large hands would open fully. The heavy warmth upon her chest slid lower to the gentle rise of her breasts.

Barely breathing, she knew she had to have him touch her.

Unable to move, she watched desire flare in his face, saw the sharp intake of his breath as his palms slid downward. He touched her with reverence, his hands trembling as they gently explored. The pleasure was almost pain, the waiting an ache.

The pads of his thumbs moved gently across the crests, arousing sensitive nubs. He closed his eyes, breathing roughly.

When she stirred, wanting to run, wanting to move against him, J.D. tightened his grasp. "How does it feel to know you can make me ache?" he asked almost bitterly, the words cutting at her.

His fingers tightened about her softness, the touch still gentle, yet possessive. "You owe me this, I think."

A ripple of excitement danced across her flesh and warmth curled inside her.

Watching her in his turn, J.D. slid the T-shirt from her. The sunlight passing through the trees dappled her breasts, and he surveyed them with such a dark, intense hunger that she shivered. "Move against me, Kat," he ordered roughly. "Let me feel you—"

The desire was so strong, igniting her own need that she leaned closer. When her softness just touched his chest, he stopped breathing. "Closer—"

The hair covering his chest brushed her sensitive breasts, the heat of his body penetrating her flesh. J.D.'s lean stomach met her softer one, his hard thighs pressing, heating—

She wanted to stop.

She wanted to take.

Katherine wanted to open her hands, to skim the steely ridges of his taut neck and the cords flowing down his arms.

She wanted to place her hot cheek against the sheathed muscle of his chest.

J.D.'s face hardened, a dark red color rising on his cheeks. He surveyed her face, letting his gaze linger on her half-closed eyes, the moist part of her lips. His eyes drifted to the pale softness that nestled against him. "I think, Miss Katherine," he said slowly, "that you and I are in one hell of a mess."

She couldn't resist the smile that tugged at his lips, nor the jaunty angle of his left eyebrow—as if he knew everything.

Well, he didn't. Not by half. J.D. didn't know that right then she needed him the way she needed air. Maybe she always had.

But J.D. had committed and been judged guilty of a crime against her pride. He'd twined himself into Irish's life, intentionally using her own sister to get to her, and Katherine was committed to her own course. For his encroachment, J.D. was sentenced to exile from the Dalton family circle.

He could make his life-influencing decisions with some-one else's relatives. Mulling the thought, Katherine allowed her eyes to drift over J.D.'s body.

A muscle crossing his chest tightened, contracting be-neath the dark skin, and she felt a ripple of sheer pleasure. She could riffle that arrogant, male pride.

Perhaps Abagail did know how to play a better game. Katherine had never thought of herself as seductive, but now the idea was enticing. There were rules and there were rules.

Katherine inched back and covered her breasts with her arms. One of her sneakers had come off, and she allowed the goo to rise between her toes. Stretching and curling them, she indulged in the totally feminine pleasure of being a woman who is attractive to a man. Of course, J.D. was definitely the wrong man. Her weakness for J.D. as a de-lectable male needed to be—she searched for the correct Western lingo—"cut off at the pass."

Allowing herself one last, tempting wriggle, Katherine asked, "Are we done with fun time, Mr. Macho? Is it time for liniment and warm soaks?"

His brows seemed to ram together, the vein running along his temple beginning to throb. "What are you talking about, Kat?"

She liked catching J.D. on his unspiked broadside. The feeling was actually quite pleasant. One to be savored. Just a little payback for being so damned sexy after all these years.

For running through her blood like hot, sweet honey.

She dissected him as though he were a chief suspect in a major crime and saw him scowl. "You're really not in the age-group to be playing caveman, you know."

J.D. looked down his nose at her like a Doberman con-templating a playful kitten. After a moment, he smiled re-luctantly. He trailed a muddy finger along her shoulder. "You're nasty, Kat. A street fighter looking for low blows."

"Mmm," she agreed lightly, searching for a way out of the bog. Catching a willow branch, she tested her footing. "Enjoy your beauty bath, J.D. I've got work to do."

"I don't think even Big Jim would want you wrapped up in his shroud on a day like this, Kat."

Turning to him, she rubbed her muddied palms, studying the elegant nails closely. "This little business venture could wind up costing you more than it's worth, J.D."

Katherine glanced at the field of white-petaled daisies swaying in the breeze. "Irish doesn't have to come into this, J.D. But so help me, if you don't back out now, I'll blow you straight out of Denver."

Easing back a wayward strand from her forehead, J.D. realized he'd rather be fighting Katherine than loving any other woman. He lifted her into his arms and stepped onto the bank. "You're a hell of a woman, Kat. But you're playing with fire. You act as if you're itching for a good fight, but maybe you're really needing something else," he warned softly against her ear.

Turning to him, Katherine's mouth was a fraction of an inch away from his. "I'm not fighting; you haven't got a thing I want."

"I've got Irish," he returned evenly, letting her slip to the ground. He brushed a drop of mud from her jaw, his thumb lingering on the hollow of her cheek. Then it slid away, leaving the area chilled. "Let me show you the acreage, Kat. You haven't really been over it all."

Beneath Katherine's protective arms, the peaks of her breasts hardened as he lowered his lashes, his gaze flowing downward. "I'm in a bargaining mood today. I'll be gone tomorrow, and you won't have another shot at me for a week. Think of it, Kat. A chance to explore my weaknesses."

Speaking in a conspiratorial tone, he added, "I'll even tell you what I found behind the madame's mirrors."

Katherine leveled a dark stare at him. "I'm not interested. Now or ever."

"Don't be so sure." With the tip of his finger J.D. eased a muddied strand of hair behind her ear. Humor lurked in his dark eyes, the lines beside them crinkling. "Take a ride with me, Kat. Irish has got some good ideas—"

She shivered, suddenly feeling hesitant. The emotion was unfamiliar to Katherine and she glanced away, not wanting J.D. to see her weakness. "I don't think—"

J.D.'s mud-splattered left eyebrow rose, mocking her. "Afraid of me, Kat?"

"Not on your life."

Travis appeared from behind the fence, his arms filled with towels and clean clothes. "Irish said to use the new bathhouse," he managed with pride.

J.D. stepped in front of Katherine, shielding her from his grandson as he took the clothes. "Okay, thanks a lot, Travis. You can go on back now."

Feeling the cool breeze touch her, the mud drying and cracking, Katherine shivered and watched Travis run back to the inn and his brownies.

Surprising her, J.D. dropped a kiss onto her nose. "Don't look so deserted. I'm still here. No one is going to see your charms."

The possessive, protective statement would ordinarily have enraged Katherine. But it was pretty hard to deal with J.D. being gallant. While she was balancing her independence against J.D.'s takeover, he sluiced himself off with a small hose. He grabbed his shirt from the privacy fence and tossed it to her. "You'd better put this on."

Katherine frowned, looking at the large, Western-cut shirt. Usually she didn't like being ordered about by anyone. She fingered the cotton cloth, tracing the standard plaid pattern and the pearl snaps. She'd never liked takeovers, and wearing J.D.'s shirt recalled the ownership he'd claimed over her years ago. Slipping behind the curtain of willow branches, she glanced at him as he scouted the scenery for intruders.

J.D. Tough, unyielding . . . tormenting, protective and . . . gentle when he touched her.

She'd loved Big Jim. Hadn't she? Unaccustomed to guilt, Katherine felt it wash over her. She'd given her husband everything. *Hadn't she?*

She trembled, just becoming aware of the weakness in her legs. She had to tear J.D. out of her life *and* Irish's. J.D. had once made a decision for her, had treated her like a child.

To come near him was like playing moth to his flame; she was certain to get singed.

Gazing over the fields, watching the cloud shadows slide across the rugged, mountainous slopes, Katherine frowned. Her hands curled into fists, crushing the cloth. She did need to know him better—to wrest Irish free.

A willow branch brushed her cheek, and Katherine smiled slowly. J.D. needed his comeuppance. She needed the fresh air and the horseback ride—and she needed to show J.D. that the past was truly dead. Ashes to ashes.

Seven

—

Katherine's eyes blazed over her shoulder as she looked at J.D. "You didn't say we were going to ride *double*, J.D."

J.D. allowed himself to savor the tight set of her mouth. Katherine off balance was beautiful, exciting and entirely delectable. "Kat, you know the sorrel mare is lame. Irish already has her in a herbal wrap," he reminded her. "Rio can carry both of us easily."

Her fingers moved restlessly on the saddle horn, following the tooled leather design as she digested his logic.

J.D. reined the big black stallion to the left, avoiding a patch of prairie dog holes. The movement brought his forearm beneath Katherine's breasts, their gentle sway caressing his flesh.

Using the pretext of guiding the horse, J.D. allowed his hard thighs to settle along the curve of her legs. His hands trembled, and J.D. realized how much it was costing him not to place his palms on those soft thighs. Katherine was like silk—the texture needed touching, but after once stroking it, the addiction would linger.

Katherine pressed her nails warningly into his arm. "Cut it out, J.D. I'm not in the mood for erotica."

He laughed then, feeling years younger. "Honey, the other night, dressed in the madame's costume, you were pure hot—"

"J.D.!" Katherine's ponytail brushed his cheek as she turned. The fine strands caught on his jaw, luring him with their texture and scent.

"What?"

Speaking through tight lips she spaced out her words. "I'd prefer you forget that incident and you know it. It's just like you to go dredging up embarrassing moments. Tight places have a tendency to make me . . . overwrought."

He chuckled and allowed the horse to graze on a clump of fescue grass. "Tight places can make anyone nervous. Any more time in that room with you, and I would have embarrassed myself."

"That's ridiculous," she snapped. "Two adults can surely share the intimacy of a room without—"

"Without?" J.D. chuckled again, noting Katherine's high flush and the way her fingers trembled as she primly smoothed her hair.

"Some of us—rational people—have the ability to contain our reactions. Not everyone operates on a base level. . . ."

Her flush heightened as J.D.'s fingertip skimmed her cheek, reminding her of her unwilling response to him.

"So romantic," J.D. drawled; he was intensely aware of the pleasure of making Katherine uncomfortable with her human emotions.

Glancing at a minipickup parked beside the dirt road, J.D. sighted a woman reporter angling her camera toward the mountain scenery. "It's a good thing that reporter wasn't snooping around then."

For an instant humor warmed Katherine's eyes. She tapped a nail against her softly pursed lips. "Now that would have been interesting. The great J. D. MacLean—"

A girl rode across the meadow before them, tall daisies swaying in the breeze around her horse's legs. Dressed in short, cutoff jeans, her long legs pressed against the horse's sides. The wind pasted the short, cotton top to her chest and lifted her ponytail. The unsaddled pony suddenly took a series of sharp turns. J.D. nodded toward her. "That's Georgia Evans. Last year she was the county's best barrel racer."

The girl waved, then began to move. The animal kept his pace even, and the girl's bare feet seemed to lock into place as she eased herself to a standing position on the horse's back. The action was daring and the girl's smile wide as they returned her wave. "She's very pretty," Katherine said, knowing that once she, too, had danced near danger.

"Fool thing to do, since this whole field is pockmarked with prairie dog holes," J.D. muttered, drawing Rio to a standstill beneath the shade of tall pines.

"She's young, and the young are sometimes reckless," Katherine observed, remembering how she'd felt when she'd first tasted J.D.

The girl held up her arms in a victorious gesture and suddenly Katherine felt very old and worn.

"Was I ever that young?" Katherine asked softly, watching the teenager ease herself back into a sitting position.

Behind her J.D. was very still. Turning her head to meet his eyes, Katherine felt his fingers slip between hers, enfolding her gently with his strength.

The touch hovered and warmed her, oddly reassuring. "She's so young, J.D."

"You were that young and every bit as reckless," he answered slowly, roughly, as though he, too, was remembering the past. "You defied a whole town to mother Daisy and see that I ate right. I heard about it often enough from the gossips. They liked you being at the house about as much as I did.''

Watching his expression, Katherine saw the same deep concern for her as she had all those years ago.

"I didn't have anything to offer you then, Kat,'' he whispered, drawing her back against his chest, fitting her within the sheltering cove of his body. "You had a whole life ahead of you."

Closing her eyes, Katherine allowed herself to rest a moment against him. She'd fought her battles and met her goals, clinging to her hatred of J.D. and using it to thrust herself through life. She'd been so hurt, but weaving through her memories was one undeniable truth. "You know, I think that in your place I might have acted the same," she admitted slowly.

Tracing circles on the back of her hand, J.D.'s thumb pressed gently into her flesh. The gesture was companionable, one of understanding between friends. But she'd hated him for years, and the thought of friendship immediately went skittering into the sumac bushes.

Reacting instantly, Katherine sat upright and moved away. In desperation she slipped her hand from his, from the symbol of possession, fitting it over the saddle horn. J.D. was stalking too closely, making her feel something that was beyond her control.

"That must have cost you." The raw depth riding his low voice mixed with the swish of the pine branches overhead and the warm, morning sun. "Well, here's one for you, Kat."

Rio shifted, lowering his head to munch on the sweet grass. J.D. tightened his grip on the loose reins, then rested his hand briefly on Katherine's. Watching the clouds caught by the wind, sweeping shadows across the blue-purple mountains and dipping into the canyons, Katherine waited, sensing that he was sorting out his thoughts. J.D. toyed with her wedding ring, twisting it gently on her finger. "Maybe I was wrong all those years ago. I just wanted more for you."

Katherine looked down at the hand that encircled her wrist. In a way he'd always bound her. She had to know. "Did you care back then?"

The air grew still; the fluttering aspen leaves waited in the silence. And then he laughed, the harsh sound startling Rio into sidestepping. J.D. easily controlled the stallion, sliding his arm around Katherine's waist to hold her safely.

Katherine turned to him, her hand raised to strike at him. "Did you, damn you?" she demanded, fighting the hot tears behind her lids.

He caught her wrist, bringing it to his mouth. His lips brushed the sensitive inner flesh as his hand splayed across her shoulders. "I cared."

He smiled slowly. At the gentleness of his expression she looked away. She didn't want the weakness that was creeping over her, the need to bury herself in him. He'd been her enemy for years and she wanted to keep it that way. "That's my Kat, clinging to her pride, no matter the cost. You can lean that stiff back against me and rest awhile," he whispered against her ear. "Whatever's riding you, give it a break. Come on," he urged, sliding his hand beneath her hair.

J.D.'s strong fingers found the tense cords in the nape of her neck and massaged them. "Atta girl, champ," he said when she stiffened and moved away.

"What do you mean?"

He ran a finger down her cheek. "Maybe I felt—for just an instant—that you needed me. Hell, maybe I needed to be needed."

There he was, dancing too close again, prying at emotions she'd rather keep buried beneath a mound of resentment. Preparing to defend herself, Katherine lifted her head and watched the strands of her hair slip and catch along the dark strength of his jaw. "Aren't you just a little bit curious after all these years, Kat?" he asked in a sensuous drawl, lowering his lips to brush hers.

The air in her lungs grew still; the pulse of her blood began to slow—

"J.D., we're both past the age of experimenting."

"Don't count on it, Kat. Somehow, between us, we manage to toss out a few rules."

The next day was sunlit and gorgeous—Katherine hated it from the moment she opened her tired eyes that morning. She'd dreamed during the night of J.D. as the gambler who had supposedly seduced Abagail and led her into an immoral life. J.D. fitted the part perfectly. And his ability to hatch diabolical schemes was increasing.

The fact that he was Travis's grandfather was a biological accident, she decided in the dawn hours. The boy was simply too sweet, laughing more each day as she worked with him to carefully script the alphabet.

At breakfast Irish was disgustingly cheerful; Katherine had to hold her breath through another Mr. Wonderful lecture about J.D. "J.D. knows his marketing stuff. And the way he'd gotten Travis to feel more a part of everything, more secure. Imagine a business potentate like J.D. taking time off to go fishing with his grandson and camping, and help us out, too."

Seated at the kitchen table, Katherine lifted the hem of her cream satin robe to cover her bare legs and studied the effect of the warm sunlight that was touching her toes. "Help *you* out," she corrected her sister. "You keep trying to shove J.D. at me, Irish, and I wouldn't come within—"

"He's a catch, Kat." Irish's hands molded the wedge-shaped figure of a man in the air. "Nice shoulders, nice smile, and he's fun, too. I'll bet he's monogamous and great in bed. And he obviously knows how to treat a lady. All sterling qualities, if you're in the market for a husband."

Katherine poured herself another hot, bracing cup of coffee. "You can stop the sales pitch. I'm certainly not in the market for anyone like J.D. Neither are you. I want to know just how far this relationship with J.D. has gone. And I want to know exactly how you got involved with him."

Irish grinned, leaning a hip against the counter and sipping her herbal tea. "Just the facts, ma'am? Could it be you're interested in him for your own purposes? And just why don't you like him? See, I know how to ask questions, too."

Wriggling her bare soles on the sun-warmed squares of linoleum, Katherine frowned at her sister. "All that bosh about Abagail is nonsense. You're up to your eyeballs in fraud, Irish. Perpetuating the memory of a madame can't be all that much fun."

"She deserves her place in history. That's what J.D. said, and he's keeping her legend alive for posterity," Irish flung back adamantly. "The stressed-out execs will love the idea. J.D. says it's a perfect marketing theme that's sure to fly."

"Bunk and horsefeathers."

"Is that a legal term?" Irish asked, a shade too innocently. She glanced out the window just as Katherine stood up, preparing to press her advantages of height and older-sister concern. "Oh, gosh. Here's J.D. and Travis. We'll have to save our talk for another time," Irish exclaimed without regret as the MacLeans entered the large, bright kitchen.

Travis offered Katherine a bouquet of wildflowers and she crouched to accept them. J.D., dressed in a cotton shirt and jeans, looked at the gap in her robe with interest. "Morning, Kat." The sensual drawl caused her to look up from hugging Travis.

Rising slowly, she sensed the black eyes probing beneath the satin to her beige teddy. She resented every ounce of the answering attraction within her. No man should look that delicious in a worn, pink shirt and jeans that molded his long legs. The shirt gaped across his chest, exposing a thick thatch of hair.

She remembered that hair and turned back to Travis to hide the blush that was creeping up her cheeks. J.D. had that roguish look—the wind-rumpled hair, the strong, un-shaven jaw and wicked, wicked eyes. "Kat is pretty in the morning, isn't she, Travis?" he asked. She felt his gaze stroll down her body.

Refusing to slide away, Katherine lifted her head. If he wanted to play male predator, he could do it with women other than Irish and herself.... Her heart skipped a beat. Did he play hungry male with Irish?

The sharp pang of jealousy—and regret—surprised her.

"I like Kat," Travis stated firmly. "Do you want some guppies, Kat?"

"Travis is talking more and leaning how to share, Kat," J.D. murmured softly. "Thanks to you."

J.D.'s gaze held hers, and Katherine realized slowly that she was holding the little boy's hand like a lifeline. Without moving, J.D. bent and brushed his mouth across her own.

The light contact went singing through her, leaving her hot and hungry.

She wanted to run.

Irish cleared her throat. "Ah...Kat, could you get me some raspberry jam from the pantry?"

Katherine backed away from J.D. and his slow, knowing grin. He'd reached straight into her heart without giving fair warning. Nothing about the man was fair, she decided as she quickly entered the spacious pantry.

She tugged the string that hung from the overhead bulb, but nothing happened.

The floorboards creaked behind her and Katherine tugged again. "Irish, nothing in this place works. It's going to cost a fortune to have the electricity rewired, and you can stop throwing that carpetbagger at me every time I turn around."

"Why don't you turn around and tell me yourself, Kat?" J.D. drawled.

Katherine jumped back against the wall at his sudden proximity. The door slammed shut and she was alone with him in the dark. For a moment she listened to the heavy sound of her own breathing and the beating of her heart.

Then she gripped the old doorknob and rattled it with all her might. "Irish!"

"Carpetbagger?" The softly spoken question was louder than the silence from the kitchen.

She threw out a hand in a protective gesture, and it landed in the center of a very hard, warm chest. She wanted her safe, spacious, well-lighted courtrooms and her greasy slum landlords. Okay, she'd even take obnoxious, chauvinistic judges and jurists worrying not about the case, but about the daily menu. "I can't see. Don't come near me."

"What an invitation—you won't know where to hit," he returned; she felt his heat seep through her light clothing.

Katherine backed away a step, the pantry shelves hard at her back. "I'll wing it. Maybe I'll hit something vital," she threatened, feeling the room close in on her. She was cold and sweating now, trembling with the fear of being trapped in a small place.

Nervously she rubbed her palms together and discovered them to be cold and clammy. Katherine scowled in the approximate direction of J.D.'s head. Then she found she had perpetrated the unforgivable crime by inching fractionally toward his warmth.

"Irish and Travis are changing the herbal wrap on the mare's leg," J.D. observed with a trace of humor. "And that leaves you with me."

"Hah!" Now her head was swimming. "That will be a cold day in—"

His hand felt large as it framed her cheek. "We could be stuck in here until afternoon," he added. "Abagail must be prowling around, doing her ghostly work."

"Noon." her husky voice echoed the ominous deadline. She couldn't possibly shield her fear from him until then. She knew she was holding his wrist with one hand, but couldn't seem to let go. "You know as well as I do that Irish has booby-trapped this money pit," she muttered absently.

She heard him shift in the darkness, and Katherine's hand shot out to grasp the safety of his cotton shirt. He was her enemy, but he wasn't leaving her alone in the abyss. "Did you lock us in here purposely?"

"Ouch! Of course not." He inhaled sharply and tugged her wrist away from his chest. "Watch it, Kat. I'm fragile."

She missed the humor, struggling not to throw herself into his arms. At least he was safer than the darkness around her, even if it was scented with spices, apples and laundry soap. "I just hate closed places. I can't breathe," she admitted.

Waiting for his mockery, Katherine wiped her hand across her forehead and found it damp. She'd been trapped in a playhouse for hours as a child, and now the old fears came surging back. Shivering, she discovered a large, warm hand cupping her shoulder. "Come here." The soft order left her no alternative but to step into his arms.

She shuddered, feeling his safety wrap around her. "This is awful," she muttered against his chest, relaxing slightly as his hand smoothed her hair. "Do you think Irish got rid of *all* the mice?"

"The exterminator was first-class, Angel. The only living things in this pantry are you and me...and it is awful," he repeated against her forehead. "I can't wait to get out." The statement lacked conviction.

Still shivering, Katherine slid her arms around his waist. She had no choice, really. J.D. was the only living, safe object in the room. Fighting her fears, she held on to J.D. and searched for something to fling at him—he was guilty of witnessing her lack of control and therefore needed taking down. Trying to see his face, her cheek grazed a rough patch of stubble. "You've got to quit encouraging Irish to promote Abagail. And you've got to leave her alone. She's not up to being—"

"God help me. I want you, Kat." The quiet statement fell into the darkness like a blazing arrow shooting into the night.

Before she could answer, his lips moved along her throat. She turned to protest and his mouth locked against hers; his tongue slipped intimately inside.

Katherine absorbed the shock, tried to rally for a struggle—and somehow went sailing into her own violent needs. He cupped the back of her head, fingers massaging her scalp as he deepened the kiss. "Hold on, Angel," he murmured, the name a sweet endearment now. "I'll take care of you."

"J.D." Was her husky voice protesting or welcoming? she wondered fleetingly as his large, warm hands swept the robe from her.

She shook helplessly as he slipped the teddy's tiny straps from her shoulders, feeling the heat and the anticipation explode within her. When the teddy fell silkily to the floor, J.D.'s rough hands moved down her body, exploring it with a trembling reverence that shocked her.

"Put your arms around my neck," he whispered against her hot cheek. "Trust me."

"Oh, no," she heard herself exclaim as he took off his shirt. She didn't want to touch her mouth to his chest. But his deep, ragged groan had her completing the task. "J.D., do something—"

For answer he groaned again, then fitted his palms beneath her bottom to lift her higher. Her arms tightened around his neck just as his mouth found her left breast. The impact of his hot, moist lips tugging on her sent another stunning wave of heat racing through her.

Katherine felt his full arousal fit snugly against her, and her lower body ached.

He suckled at her breast in a rhythm that made her gasp. Needing him, Katherine ran her fingers through his hair to guide him to her other breast. She could feel herself opening, flying through space as small ripples began deep within her.

When his teeth gently worried her nipple, Katherine forgot everything but him and the excitement that was racing uncontrolled between them.

Stunned, she caught the white-hot heat within her and trembled as she placed her flushed face against the safety of his throat.

Breathing heavily, he slipped his fingers slowly into her moist, intimate depths. The delicate invasion started another, deepening series of sensual contractions.

He held her as the passion rode on. His dark, urgent whispers carried her through the storm, taking her ever higher. Katherine began to bloom. She felt herself tighten, first riding the bursting passion, then slipping quietly into a warm, dark heaven.

Barely aware of movement, she clung to him, allowing him to bestow soft kisses upon her hot face. When she roused, feeling weak and drowsy, she felt J.D.'s hands soothing her, heard his hushed encouragement gradually bring her back to reality. He was seated on the floor, cradling her in his lap.

Helplessly she leaned back to stare at him. She'd never felt as safe as in these shadows. He carefully covered her with her robe and nuzzled her cheek, the stubble grazing her damp skin. "Better? I hope so, because I definitely have a problem now."

Beneath her he was fully aroused. He nibbled her bottom lip, then rubbed her nose with his own. "The courtesy is to return the favor, Angel. I wouldn't object, although I think we had better wait for a door that can be locked from the inside."

"This is awful," she whispered, shocked at the savagery she felt racing through her. Trembling anew, she tried to free herself, only to find J.D.'s arms locked tighter about her.

"If you know what's good for you, you'll sit absolutely still," he muttered ominously. "There's control. Then there's control. Right now I want nothing more than to sink into that sweet, tight body of yours."

She shifted to a more comfortable spot and he reacted instantly, cursing. His teeth settled into her earlobe just far enough to make his point. When she shivered unexpectedly and moved again, to turn against him fully, he made a low, warning sound at the back of his throat. "We're on a delicate line here, Kat. You should be experienced enough to recognize that. Sit still and we'll talk—got it?" he demanded tightly.

He shook violently, and without thinking, she skimmed her hand across his shoulder. "God, Kat. Have mercy," he growled, gathering her closer. Despite the tension that was racing around them, Katherine realized rather smugly that J.D. held her as gently as a baby. As though she was a woman he prized.

Closing her eyes and resting her head upon his shoulder, she wanted the moment to last and last. Actually she liked the hard padding of his shoulders, covered by warm, dark skin.

"Stop touching me," he ordered curtly, and she realized that she had been gently stroking him. Sighing, she snuggled down, leaving J.D. to fend off the monsters of the darkness and her fears.

In times of need he was a man to be trusted.

Still drowsy, she realized that she was tired of taking on the world's ills alone. Even a crusader needed a well-padded shoulder to lay her cheek upon.

Katherine nuzzled that shoulder, enjoying the way his heart beat safely beneath her cheek.

"None of that . . . and don't go to sleep. I want to talk." The flat statement set off a tiny alarm in her senses. "You're going to tell me all about your marriage to Big Jim. And cut the bull."

When she stiffened, fighting once more for control, J.D.'s hands tightened on her arms. Shifting gears back to reality, Katherine knew that once J.D. learned the nature of her marriage to Jim, there would be real trouble. While J.D.'s lovemaking incited a major revolt in her, her emotions for Big Jim had been almost sisterly. "Back off, J.D.," she said more calmly than she felt. "I don't have to tell you a damn thing."

"You're highly flammable, Kat," he returned, brushing a thumb across her nipple, which hardened instantly. "Does wonders for my ego."

Pushing his hand away, she glared at him in the dark. "Your ego doesn't need stroking. It's King-Kong-sized already. I'm not up to a replay of your scenario, J.D. Just let me go."

"*My* scenario? You were with me all the way. If we made love fully, the place would go up in flames. Did you feel that way with Big Jim?" he asked roughly, drawing her tightly, possessively against his chest.

She didn't want to answer him. In the pause that followed he kissed her gently. "That's exactly what I thought. We're in trouble. Bad trouble."

Silence fell, and Katherine tried to find the road to sanity. A road without the undeniable delights of J.D.'s aroused body.

The thought of sliding her fingers along the insistent bulge that pressed intimately against her had her shivering once more.

Why him? She echoed the thought aloud. "Why you?"

"Why you?" he returned easily, covering her bare shoulder with the satin robe. He caressed her with his fingertips, rubbing circles on her tense back. "Why didn't you have children with him?"

The raw question made her tense. "That's my business."

J.D. laughed shakily, taking her chin into his hand. He raised her face for a tender kiss. "If you were my wife all those years, we'd have kids. Trust me."

As if to deepen and hold the thought, his hand spanned the satin, gently kneading the soft stomach beneath. "It would take a woman like you to tame any wild MacLean boys—"

Boys? Little, black-haired cowboys, each with endearing, long lashes. The thought lingered and held, grew sweet—and Katherine firmly pushed it and his hand away. She pulled the wistful curve of her lips into a straight line. "There's absolutely no reason to go strolling through all this now—"

"There isn't?" The tip of J.D.'s tongue followed the contours of her lips. The stark hunger stalled her instantly.

Swallowing the tight wad of emotion in her throat, Katherine managed to whisper, "This is all rhetorical...after-the-fact supposition—"

He chuckled, shifting her to bury his face against her throat. "Hardly. Without thought, we both could get caught—"

"Oh, my!" The idea of a child went whipping through her, unbidden and hopelessly sweet.

"Yes. Oh, my," he repeated in a rich, humorous tone. "I wish I could see your face. Your eyes are expressive. When we make love, I'll want the lights on."

Just as Katherine thought her heart had stopped beating, the screen door slammed and Irish called, "We're back."

J.D. cursed, carefully setting Katherine on her feet and moving away from her. She shivered again, missing his warmth, and heard the rasp of cloth as he replaced his shirt. "I'm holding the doorknob. Get dressed."

"Where are you guys?" Irish wanted to know.

"Grandpa? Kat?" Travis yelled. Katherine found her robe and jammed her arms into the sleeves. She wrapped the sash about her just as Irish returned to the kitchen, calling their names in her turn.

When Katherine approached the door, J.D. scooped her up for a kiss that left her breathless. "I need something to hold me over. Kiss me back and mean it," he ordered in a harsh whisper. "Or I'll tell the world how hot you really are."

"J.D.," she began angrily. "You can go hang—"

"Freedom for a kiss. Take your pick."

Feeling his hard body nearby, Katherine decided that J.D. should suffer. Reaching for his head, she leaned against him and drew his mouth to hers. Parting her lips, she deepened the kiss aggressively, throwing into it every bit of hunger she had experienced. She wanted to leave him aching, burned to a crisp. She wanted him to know that she could meet him on any level and leave him in her dust.

But there in the depths she forgot to draw back...and moved deeper into the sensual waters, letting herself flow against his larger, harder frame.

"Mmm." J.D.'s tone was deep and purely carnal; his hand circled her back to caress one breast.

Somehow, she realized as the room grew suddenly hot and her weakness returned, J.D. had turned the tables.

Irish rattled the pantry door. "Stop playing hide-and-seek. I know you're in there. Abagail must have decided that you two needed—"

Her words were lost as J.D. fitted his hand neatly over Katherine's breast.

Working herself free, she gripped the robe tightly about her trembling body, and muttered, "Hands off."

"I think," he said carefully, "that we had better think about getting asbestos sheets."

His sweet kiss effectively sealed her outraged gasp, then he firmly set her aside. "Irish, how many times have I told you to have these doors fixed?" J.D. asked with mock severity when he opened the door.

Stepping past him, Katherine avoided Irish's prying, quick eyes. Keeping her head high, she walked with as much dignity as she could manage to the staircase.

"She's shy," she heard J.D. say lightly.

Katherine flinched. Of course it was funny to him. He hadn't just discovered another side of himself.

He wasn't wondering what had happened at fever pitch.

He wasn't blushing or wondering if there were faint chafing marks on his delicate skin.

What had happened to her?

Then Irish asked casually, "Biting necks these days, is she?"

Wanting to forget, Katherine closed her eyes and held on to the banister to steady her weakened legs. Then she fled the scene, ascending the stairs at a run with her robe flowing behind her. She'd been hungry. Now she remembered how she had bitten his neck lightly to keep from crying out her passion.

Shivering slightly, she remembered too how her nails had found his shoulders. She'd needed him to anchor her in the flames, to keep her burning with his touch.

She'd needed him.... "No," she said aloud. "No, I definitely don't need J. D. MacLean."

When she reached her room and had safely closed the door, Katherine flung herself onto the bed and jerked the pillow over her head.

Much later she discovered that she had put on her robe inside out. And she hadn't taken the time to slip into her teddy. No doubt Irish had already found the incriminating evidence and would exploit it to the hilt.

Katherine groaned for the hundredth time and tried without success to slip into her private stream.

Eight

———

"She must have left at dawn. But her note said she'd call and that she'd be back, J.D.," Irish told J.D. the next morning as she slid a plate of fruit and granola toward him.

"My grandpa will get Kat back," Travis announced proudly, wiping a buttery, blueberry muffin crumb from his mouth. Talking much more freely now, Travis chattered away. "My grandpa says we MacLean men don't let our women hightail it out when the going gets rough. We make 'em stand and fight. My grandpa says—"

J.D. riffled Travis's hair, then gathered the small, pajama-clad body sitting on his lap closer. "That's enough, scout. Irish could be a spy for the women's side," he whispered in a conspiratorial tone. "Let's not give all our secrets away, hmm?"

Irish refilled J.D.'s coffee cup. "I won't tell, but what else did your grandpa say, partner?"

J.D.'s eyebrows rose warningly. "Basically I shot off my mouth, when little ears weren't supposed to be awake and listening."

He slipped his free hand into his suit pocket, grasping the beige teddy in his fist. Barely awake after a bad night, he'd heard Katherine's Jeep rev up.

"Grandpa says she's running for cover and it won't do her any good."

"Travis. That is enough." Everything J.D. had muttered to himself before he thought his grandson was awake was true. Katherine owed him, every last—

"And when my grandpa finds Kat, he's going to do...something...to her orn..." The boy struggled with the word. "Ornery hide."

Irish giggled and J.D. glared at her. His fiercest, most devastating, female-shrinking glare. Irish continued to laugh until the tears rolled down her cheeks. "I knew it," she crowed. "I just knew it when Kat ran out. You've got her on the run, J.D. It's about time."

"What do you know about it?" he demanded, noting that Travis had started to squirm. "Go to the bathroom, Travis. I won't leave for Denver until we say our goodbyes. Go on now."

When they were alone, Irish grinned. "Take your time. Travis and I are going to start visiting the neighbors today."

J.D. leveled his no-nonsense, business look at her. "You know I have to fly back and forth to Denver on business, anyway. I might visit your sister. Or I might not."

He knew damn well that after Katherine's reactions to him and the hard night he'd spent, he'd track her down and wave the beige teddy like a flag.

He tried to ignore Irish's muffled giggle. When he couldn't, he glared at her once, then moodily sipped his coffee. He brooded about how he might strip Katherine of every last defense. He wanted those sweet, almost shy kisses, the trembling, hot way she responded to his touch. He wanted—

He wanted the caring woman who had brought love back into Travis's eyes. He wanted the laughing woman of the beauty bog and the steamy passion he'd just uncovered.

Irish bent to kiss his cheek. "Something pretty interesting must have happened in the pantry. Kat didn't notice her robe was inside out. It's a good thing that Abagail is trying to take care of you two, or you might never get together."

J.D. snorted. "Abagail. No doubt you helped out just to watch the sparks fly."

Irish grinned wickedly. "Maybe. But Kat's having a hard time now, you know."

"I could tell her a lot about hard times."

"Mmm. But you see, she's just discovering she's not immune to you, J.D.," Irish added softly and sat back to savor his stunned expression.

"Did she tell you that?" J.D. shot back, ready to punch holes in Irish's theory.

"Trust me. Be gentle," she advised as Travis came padding back into the room.

"You set this up," J.D. muttered when he could talk again. The emotions tumbling through him had to be waded into slowly—

"Guilty as charged," Irish admitted blithely. "I've never seen two such hard-headed people who needed each other more. Katherine was on the edge of collapse, and you were in danger of becoming a crusty old hermit. So I simply devised a little plan. You guys needed a nudge, and I just used myself as bait. Happens all the time."

Lifting an eyebrow at her, J.D. shook his head. "She won't be happy with you."

"She'll love me anyway, and that should give you food for thought. Don't forget Travis's guppies and the alphabet letters Kat wanted him to do. She'll want them."

And me? J.D. asked himself. He realized that his hand was trembling. But she was on the run now and that was a good sign. He didn't intend to show mercy.

He'd been hungry for her for years. Suddenly he was aware of it. And now he wanted everything.

J.D. ran the flat of his hand across his jaw and found himself grinning foolishly.

Late that afternoon, Katherine lifted her stockinged feet to her desk, placing them in the center of the sunlit square. She wriggled them, enjoying the freedom from her business pumps.

She had plenty of work waiting. Evan, a legal associate, wanted a conference with her. Mandy needed to work with her schedule, wedging in time for Irish's grand opening. A shopping mall developer was threatening to bulldoze an elderly woman's house.... The list went on.

Her nails scored the mauve-upholstered chair. But what about *her* needs? she thought, remembering how she had trembled in J.D.'s arms.

Why him? she asked herself for the thousandth time. Evan, for instance, had asked her out, and she hadn't been a bit interested.

J.D. was just too...ornery to be brushed off, she decided finally. He needed taking down.

She wriggled her pink-tipped toes, firmed her lips and snapped her seventh pencil in two. Scowling at the small pile of fragments, Katherine reached for another whole one. Thinking about J.D. presented a real hazard when she was in the midst of several priority projects.

She'd run from him at dawn and she hated him for it. She grimaced and broke the new pencil.

He'd seen her weaknesses, her lack of control, and she hated him for that, too. He'd seen her cry. Worst of all, he'd shown compassion and tenderness.

What was worse than that, she thought darkly, *she had definitely responded.*

Jabbing the intercom to Mandy, Katherine asked sharply, "Are we on a tight budget or something? Get some pencils in here."

"Yes, ma'am. " Mandy's tone was too knowing. "You have a visitor—"

J.D. strolled through her office door, dressed in a business suit and wearing a devastating grin. Her heartbeat accelerated unaccountably at the sight of him. "Howdy, Miss Katherine," he said in a low, sensuous tone that started her head swimming.

Maybe she was coming down with the flu. It was going around Denver, she'd heard.

Scooting her feet off the desk, Katherine tucked them safely into the shadows.

A warning went skittering through her stunned brain. Beware of sexy cowboys bearing plastic sacks of guppies and huge bouquets of roses and daisies. Beware of dark eyes. And of the lock being turned on her office door....

As he walked toward her, she thought of the locked pantry door and the slight abrasion of his chest against hers.

She wanted to shout at him, to accuse him of breaking and entering. She'd add a hefty assault charge to the list—

Would he touch her? When? How?

The memory of his long, dark fingers sliding intimately into her sent heat pulsing through her. She stood absolutely still, bracing herself against the desk, curling her toes in the carpeting.

Why her enemy?

Where was Big Jim's safe memory? Why did she feel as if she were adrift and alone on a high mountain mesa, her past behind her, the future waiting? Then J.D. grinned rakishly and she stopped questioning.

Katherine swallowed, watching him carefully place the guppy sack on the files that littered her desk. J.D. tossed the beautiful bouquet at her and when she caught it, he scooped her into his arms.

Before she had a chance to think again, he'd managed to grip her wrists and seat himself in her desk chair. With her on his lap.

His black eyes went flicking over her face, then he kissed her. "I thought you were a fighter," he said slowly, watching her. "Why did you run?"

He was too close, prowling through her privacy as though he had that right.

"Get out." She tested his grip on her wrists and found it gentle, but unyielding. While she was doing that, his other hand moved to massage her left insole; a sneaky tactic, she decided.

"Never run from a hunter. He'll track you down," he advised softly. "So you ran right back to Big Jim's mansion, scurried around for a few hours in the safety of musty memories, then marched your sweet self back into this safe hole," he accused her.

"Stop playing with my toes!" She made an attempt to escape his sensuous fingers, trying to reach her intercom, but he was faster.

Snaring her against him, J.D. murmured against her ear, "Shh. Those guppies have had a hard day. There's a lot of turbulence over Denver. Stress is bad for them. Let's just talk quietly until the aquarium arrives, then you can yell all you want. By the way, Travis is fine. He sent you a whole sheet of perfect *A*s. He's working on his numbers, too, and he's stopped sucking his thumb."

Katherine shuddered when his teeth went gently nipping down the length of her throat. "J.D., exactly what are you doing...here?"

"I came to return your lingerie, and then to court you," he whispered in a tone that sent her thoughts splintering in all directions.

He was not only demented. J.D. was really and truly confused, she decided as he looked at her tenderly. Because he was absolutely ruthless—heartless, she told herself as he foraged for her teddy, kissed it and tossed the slinky puff onto her desk.

"Court me?" she repeated blankly as the heat beat through her. Staring at the teddy, she could feel the slow flush on her throat work its way upward.

"I didn't want it and neither did you. But neither of us are running away, are we?"

He looked at her mouth the way Travis looked at brownies—the ones with walnut halves buried in the chocolate frosting. "Courting is probably an old-fashioned way of putting it, but where you're concerned, that's how I want it. I'm expecting a fight. But I intend to get my way. You couldn't respond to me like you do if you didn't feel something, and that's good enough for now. I'm just putting you on notice."

"Notice?" she said as he lowered his head.

Against her mouth J.D. whispered roughly, "You're mine, you know. It's just working out the details from now on. For a starter I want you out of that shrine to Big Jim. I won't help you. You'll have to make every decision about what to keep and what not. But I won't have any reminders of him anywhere near our bed."

Katherine blinked once before she could speak. "You think you can come into my office and start laying out rules?"

Crushing the bouquet between them, his kiss was long and thorough. Overwhelmed by the scents of roses and J.D., Katherine found herself drowning in the sweetness of the moment. When it was gone, Katherine looked at him helplessly.

She groaned once, quietly as she flicked her tongue over her swollen lips. They tasted like him.

Grinning and looking totally pleased with himself, J.D. nodded. He placed the flowers on the desktop, as if signifying that things were progressing according to schedule. "There. Now that I have your attention, how about having dinner with me? We'll talk about getting Irish out of my clutches.''

If only he hadn't mentioned her baby sister, Katherine thought, she would have thrown J.D. out of her office on his ear. Instead, when he carefully placed her on her feet, she nodded. By dinner she'd have a plan. She just needed some thinking space. But she wouldn't run; she'd fight him this time.

"Did you lock my door when you came in?" she asked carefully, walking toward the escape route on weakened legs.

She unlocked the door as J.D. rose, stretched to his full height and glanced around her office. "Uh-huh. You were my prisoner. Where should we put the guppy tank?"

"I'm surprised you're asking my opinion. You seem to have everything else planned," she snapped, watching him warily. Give J.D. an edge and he'd sweep everything before him, she reflected, just as he loomed over her.

Cupping her chin in his hand, J.D. smiled. It wasn't a nice smile. "You're obviously not the romantic that most women are. Workaholics usually aren't. You have to be hit straight between the eyes to notice anything but your causes, Kat. We'll give it time."

When Katherine jerked her head away and swatted at his hand, his expression darkened. "Damn it, Kat. I'm trying—"

"You're making decisions for me, and I won't have it."

"The hell you won't," he growled, reaching for her.

A brief knock on the oak panel was just the excuse she needed. Frowning at J.D., she jerked open the door. "Come in."

Evan Drobinski walked into her office, slapping a file against his well-molded thigh. His blond hair was rakishly styled, and his dark blue eyes were shooting between J.D. and herself. By the expression on his handsome face, he was clearly assessing the tension racing between them.

If she hadn't been so upset, Katherine would have found the situation amusing.

She saw Evan run a slow, questioning stare over her mussed hair, high coloring and well-kissed lips. His eyes found her furious ones and he asked, "Is there a problem, Katherine?"

She could feel J.D. breathing with male possessiveness, and a happy little something went skipping through her. How silly, she thought, forcing the feeling down and using her most businesslike tone to introduce the men. "Evan Drobinski, this is J. D. MacLean. J.D., Evan."

A pulse throbbed along J.D.'s dark throat and a muscle tightened in his jaw. Katherine experienced a whimsical need to place her fingertips just over the hard cord. She clenched her hands tightly. Enemies shouldn't be touchable.

J.D. thrust out a big hand to shake the one Evan extended. The brief gesture was an instant male assessment of the opponent's power. "Drobinski. Top attorney," he said, almost growling the acknowledgment.

"MacLean," Evan returned in the same tone, then glanced at the flowers and guppies on Katherine's desk. "I've heard of you, of course."

J.D. narrowed his eyes, then strode back to her desk, collecting the sack of guppies. "I'm keeping the fish and canceling the aquarium," he said, returning to her.

Watching Evan, J.D. drew Katherine's fist to his mouth. He ran his lips across her white knuckles, visibly branding her as his woman.

While she dealt with putting all the pieces of the J.D. puzzle together and throwing the box away, he bent to give her a sizzling kiss that left her weak and breathless.

"See you tonight, Angel. Rest up—it'll be a late one." Then he winked knowingly at her, nodded at Evan, and left the office, whistling, "You Are My Sunshine."

J.D. watched Katherine walk toward his restaurant table. He'd deliberately chosen the most romantic, candle-lit, violin-playing night-spot available to set the scene. There wasn't a chance in hell that Big Jim would have courted Kat in this small, intimate restaurant that catered to lovers.

J.D. had called Kat's secretary within moments of making the reservations and been firm about her taking a taxi. Katherine would follow directions. She wanted him out of her life too badly.

If Evan the Doberman had brought her here, J.D. would obliterate the memory. And when he saw the blond Viking next, he'd break both his legs.

Admiring the picture she created, J.D. decided what he liked about Katherine: she'd fight for her family and her causes. The way she'd taken Travis under her wing despite J.D.'s objections had proved to be for the best. He admired the way Katherine kept their skirmishes away from the boy, obviously loving him.

But tonight wasn't about Irish and Travis. It was about a shoot-out with Katherine.

From the looks of her she knew it, too. Head held high, Katherine was dressed in a hot red silk sheath and jacket, with high-heeled shoes to match. She was fighting mad and carried herself as if she were going into a major battle.

She was. After seeing Drobinski in her office, J.D. had decided to step up the pace. He worked better at a fast speed, anyway—when he really wanted something—while Katherine apparently was a woman who needed time to think.

She could have all the time in the world to think—after they'd made love. After she was fully his, she'd be easier to tame. *Or would she?*

There really wasn't another woman for him, he thought, as she shot a hot glare at him across the room. She'd aroused some pretty heavy instincts in him...like possession, like tenderness. Like the need to share his life with her.

Had Irish really meant it when she'd said Katherine was in love with him?

What the hell would he do if Katherine made love with him, then left him to wrap Big Jim's shroud around herself?

He remembered Evan the Doberman and added another unsettling question: would she ever fall into another man's arms?

Intending to give her a memory that would wipe out anything previous, J.D. gave his full attention to the woman coming toward him.

He rose slowly as she wound her way through the clusters of small, round tables, lighted by candles. Katherine had papers in her hand, probably the ones related to Irish's debts. That was good, he thought, admiring the way she met his eyes. If she'd worked on papers for two hours, that meant she hadn't had time to think about the consequences of a few sips of wine.

Seduction wasn't a fair game, and he knew it.

He was too gut-wrenchingly scared to play by the rules. He wanted certain answers, and in her usual form she'd go down fighting, without ever giving him a slip of the truth.

After the quiet, tense spaghetti dinner, Katherine sipped her red wine and slid her papers in front of J.D. "I imagine you know what these are," she said, watching the candlelight flicker across his rugged face.

If he hadn't been J.D., she could almost have enjoyed the company. But she couldn't relax around him, not for a minute. She wanted to wrench Irish free, and J.D. seemed very accommodating tonight. She looked at him over the rim of her wineglass and wondered vaguely when it had been refilled.

Katherine glanced at him again while he listened quietly to their waiter. She had her course set to pay him back—to make him ache for her.

"Mmm," he answered, raising his hand. In seconds their table was surrounded by musicians, their violins trembling with Italian love songs. Not taking his eyes from her, J.D.

lifted her hand, turned the palm to his mouth and pressed his lips into the soft center.

Katherine felt the thrill wind straight up her arm and through her body. The black head bent so appealingly over her hand gave her a feeling of being...feminine...wanted.

His hand brushed a tendril behind her ear, and on an impulse, Katherine turned her mouth to touch his skin. J.D. tensed, his hand in midair. She saw his quick, savage frown, the trembling of his hand as it took hers.

"Katherine," he murmured quietly, and the echo beat loudly in her heart. "You and I both know that Irish is not the object of the evening."

Aware that flashbulbs were going off in the distance, Katherine found herself fighting the urge to touch J.D.'s dark hair, too. To rumple it slightly as she had when he had opened his mouth on her hand. "I agree. Later then," she murmured, wonderingly hazily why on this occasion business didn't come first.

He nibbled on her fingers one by one. "You're beautiful, Angel," he whispered, running a finger down her throat. The touch left a warm path and Katherine closed her eyes, drifting with the flow of the music and the heat of the emotions flowing through her. Opening her eyes again, she found J.D. staring at her mouth with that stark, hungry look that fascinated her. Testing the look, she licked her lips and saw him scowl.

"Kat," he rasped unevenly. "Shall we go?"

"Where?" She didn't want the romantic feeling to end. Was it possible that she actually wanted to spend time with the wolf who was at her baby sister's door?

She'd set off to tame him, hadn't she?

"My place." The deep, rumbling tone sent off warning sparks in her head, set her stomach tumbling and her hands trembling.

"Why?" Katherine couldn't draw her eyes from his dark ones, even though a camera flashed again nearby.

He raised his thick brows. "To top off a memorable occasion. Unless you're afraid. Are you?"

In his penthouse office later, Katherine knew that she was indeed afraid. Of him. And of herself.

Once the door had closed and the lock clicked shut, J.D. stripped off his coat. He tossed it onto a chair. "So this is it," he murmured quietly, watching her. "I've waited a long time for this."

"So have I," Katherine answered truthfully, taking off her jacket. She folded it carefully, then placed it beside his. Kicking off her heels, she placed her hands on her hips.

Throwing caution into the night, she stated, "I was exhausted and barely in control earlier. But I'm stronger now and I can fight back."

"Ah, the awaited threat . . . and you were out of control. That admission must have cost. So you were human. You got tired."

His taunts were deliberate; she felt his eyes flickering over her. "Not functioning properly, I could have cost my clients," she told him between her teeth.

"To you that would have been the mortal sin of all time, the final disgrace. But I understand. I shouldn't have shot off my mouth about you not having human frailties. I have a few myself. Years ago I almost drank myself to death because of you."

While she was dealing with that, he flicked open the buttons of his shirt. "Has Evan ever made love to you?"

She blinked, trying unsuccessfully to follow the direction of his thought. "Evan? He's a business associate."

"He's circling, biding his time."

"You're demented," she returned, tilting her head to one side. "Evan doesn't think of me that way."

He laughed; now she saw his eyes studying the length of her. "He's a man, isn't he? After the pantry lock-in, it's a wonder I'm not crazy."

Katherine dug her toes into the thick carpeting. "I knew you'd bring that up. Low blows are your style. You just wait for moments to pounce."

"Like this one," he answered, swinging her into his arms and walking toward his bedroom.

He tossed her onto his bed and followed her down. Katherine's breath went out of her with a soft whoosh. When she could breathe again, she became aware that J.D. was looking at her with hungry interest—a predator waiting for his prey to move.

Holding herself still beneath the heavy weight of his body, Katherine felt a sudden urge to wrap her arms around him and hold on, no matter what. Instead she forced herself to clench the cocoa-colored velvet spread beneath her. "You're too old to face charges of rape," she said quietly, listening to his heart race against her. "I could ruin you."

"Before you leave here I intend to have the answers to long-overdue questions." His gaze shot greedily over the silvery strands of hair spread across the dark brown velvet. "And I don't care how I get them. If you're counting on chivalry now—don't."

A heavy thigh moved insistently along her leg, deliberately caressing the red silk higher, but Katherine wouldn't give him the satisfaction of seeing her shiver in response. She fought the wild impulse to touch her lips to the savagely pulsating vein along his throat. "I cut my legal teeth on men who forced themselves—"

His smile wasn't nice. "Forced?" He moved slightly, turning his tanned throat for her to see. "As for teeth, you've already used them. Your nails are sharp, too."

She breathed quietly, hating the heat that was pouring through her. *He'd been her enemy for years. Why him?* she asked herself once more, desperately now, as his hand moved to stroke her thigh. Somehow her flesh was warming to his touch, waiting for it; she had almost lifted her hips to his.

"That's it, Kat," he whispered roughly. "Let's see how damned long you can control this situation."

Offering her no comforting whispers, no gentle touch, J.D. placed his mouth up on hers. The kiss was hot and savage, igniting what had been waiting in her.

When it was done, the small straps at Katherine's shoulders had been torn by strong hands, the zipper had been tugged down. Slowly she realized that the dress was being drawn over her head.

She clung to it for a moment, pitting herself against his strength before his mouth once more sank onto hers.

Shaking violently, Katherine felt his mouth ease more gently around hers; a deep, reluctant growl came from his throat. Taking her wrists, J.D. placed her hands upon his chest. "You're on your own, Angel," he murmured, his teeth nipping gently at her earlobe. "You're going to ask me nicely."

"So kind," she managed shakily, realizing that somehow he had slipped off his shirt and that her fingers were eagerly foraging through warm, crisp hair.

"Lower," he demanded unevenly, unsnapping her garters to ease her stockings from her.

"No." Somehow the husky denial didn't sound quite firm, even in her own ears.

"You will," he murmured while his fingers prowled along the delicate lace briefs to stroke her gently, intimately.

"Won't!" she gasped as he stripped off his slacks and briefs.

"Will," he insisted, shifting downward to kiss the gentle slope of her breasts. Tugging the lingerie from her, he slipped his hand between her legs, urging them apart.

Katherine fought the intimacy; her body shook as J.D. found her with his touch. "Oh... Please—" But as the hunger caught her, bound her and took her into a rippling, hot tide, she found herself crying out his name.

Before she could recover and defend herself, J.D. was over her, pressing her into the bed, his expression savage. "I want to know and now, damn it, if you felt this with him, Kat," he demanded angrily.

He was tense, damp with sweat, trying to control his emotions, she realized distantly. Her hands smoothed his arms, moved to his lean waist and caressed the small of his back. At her touch J.D. thrust against her. "Damn it. Quit that. Tell me—"

Fighting the hot tears behind her lids, Katherine opened her eyes. This was a time for truth, no matter what tomorrow would bring. She'd fought him for years, but for tonight she would yield to the inevitable.

In the morning there would be no excuses. She wanted this, had waited and hungered for the moment J.D. would come for her.

She wanted J.D. to hold her.

She'd been too lonely, too long.

But he asked too much. He wanted her soul. A tear slipped quietly down her cheek. "Don't—"

"You didn't sell yourself, did you, Kat?" he suddenly wanted to know, trembling above her. "I've stayed up nights, thinking about it. You didn't use me to take your virginity," he continued, saving her the admission. "You gave yourself to me because you wanted to, and I threw it right back in your face. I hurt you."

When she looked at him helplessly, knowing her emotions were scrawled across her face, J.D.'s firm mouth curved into a soft smile.

"No answer? Let me give you one. You were hurt back then, striking out any way you could. I've watched you with Irish and Travis for weeks now, and you know exactly how to show your feelings with them. But when I get too close, you get nervous. You start using your claws."

Lowering her eyelids, Katherine bit her lip and tasted blood. He was too close to her now, pressing and raking away at old wounds. "Go to—"

"You wanted to put me through hell and you did," he said, interrupting her curse. "You're going to pay with your sweet hide, Kat."

"I won't give you what you want," she said quietly, turning to him.

"Of course you will. And more," he returned, carefully lowering his chest against her.

"No." But his kiss was so soft and warm that Katherine accepted it without hesitation. She pressed her face against the security of his throat and held on to the broad shoulders.

"Touch me," he muttered against her hot cheek.

When she curled her fingers into his side, J.D. took her hand.

She didn't want to trace the smooth length, to know again the shape and feel of him. He was shaking now, breathing roughly. His hands ran restlessly along her hips and thighs, caressing, seeking and warming on their trail to her intimate depths. When he touched her, she cried out. "How long as it been, Kat?"

She found the tense cord in his throat and opened her lips over it, feeling the tempo of his pulse increase. "Coward," she heard him murmur, laughter in his tone.

While J.D. prepared to protect her, Katherine felt herself grow hot. The time had come. She shivered.

When he moved again, she closed her legs tightly, keeping him from her, then heard herself utter the words she had never said to another person. "I'm so afraid."

Stroking her thighs, his body thrusting and hard against her, he paused. "So am I."

Then she looked up at him, dark hair falling across his brow and his face intent. Katherine felt her eyes widening as her body accepted the conquering thrust of his.

Filling her, letting her adjust to him, J.D. lowered his lips to hers. Breathing unevenly, he gently bit her lip. "Trust me, Katherine. There's more."

She would remember him later, she knew. Remember the savage urgency of his touch, remember the searing heat between them.

She'd remember when he was gone and tomorrow came.

For now there was just the dark, sweet night, waiting to be filled with J.D.'s lovemaking.

Katherine closed her eyes and turned her face into his shoulder, savoring the need that was growing within her, the tender stroking of his hands across her breasts. She'd waited for years, and now the time had come to ride the storm. J.D. was shivering with passion, fighting it, allowing her time to move into the storm or leave him alone in the cold.

She'd fought him for too many years and lonely nights.

"You rat," she whispered finally against his damp shoulder, then bit him.

He jerked back a little, paused, then chuckled richly against her ear, returning the bite on her lobe. "So it's going to be like that, is it? My dear, I am shocked."

Reckless now, Katherine grinned back at him. She rubbed her insole along his bulky calf, allowing her knee to slide over his. "It's like that."

Their eyes met and held, silent words and promises flowing between them. Then he cupped her breasts, watching her.

She arched her back against the circling caresses of his thumbs. There was definitely more to life than winning cases and setting legal precedents.

"Kat," he warned as he thrust deeper within her. "You're really going to pay for this."

"Promises, promises," she whispered, then he lowered his mouth to her breasts.

The storm came quickly. She sighed, rising on the tip of the heat, seeking, driving toward the swirling need that encompassed her. J.D. breathed heavily against her throat, his deep voice ragged with a soaring passion that shot through her. "Katherine . . . my Kat, my love—"

She'd needed the passion, the heat and the tenderness that were rising between them. They brought her nourishment, pleasured her and made her ache for more. The incredible sweetness of giving herself to him was her quickening race. Locked to her, J.D. whispered—wild words, words of claiming, need and longing. She was his heart, a part of his body. A rough sound was torn from her then; the pinnacle sharpened as he clasped her closer, his hands tender as she began to dissolve.

Moments later, lying on J.D.'s chest, Katherine found her limbs weighted with sleep; now she needed only to be held and stroked and whispered to in the night.

She'd found her peace at last, she thought as she slipped into a deep sleep with J.D.'s easy breath sweeping across her cheek.

The second time the storm came quickly, taking her before she was fully awake. J.D., resting lightly upon her, filled her completely, setting off tiny ripples of pleasure. His lips captured the soft sound of her surprise and absorbed it. His mouth explored hers, the tip of his tongue playing along the contours of her parted lips.

He moved deeply within her. She enfolded him tightly, savoring the roughness of his thighs. "You're mine now," he whispered, capturing and stilling her tormenting hands.

"Yes," she cried out, drawing him still deeper.

Katherine moved desperately against him, cherishing the sensuous surge of muscle and heat. Cherishing the moment of being a woman being loved by the man she'd craved for years.

She waited for the caress of his rough palms against her breasts, the aching deep within her already cresting as he began to move. She clung to his rippling shoulders, feeling the throbbing that stalked her.

How long had she waited to be claimed? How long had she wanted to be needed?

The petals within her captured the sweet emotion and folded it gently away.

His kiss claimed and wooed and still demanded more. She gave herself to the rhythm of their passion.

"Oh, Kat. It's always been you," he whispered, riding the crest of the wave.

Nine

J.D. breathed slowly, willing the dawn to wait over Denver. During the night Katherine had given herself to him four times—or had he taken her?

He stroked Katherine's long back gently, feeling her nestle closer. The warm, luscious scents of their lovemaking curled about him, and J.D. quietly breathed them in. He wanted to keep the world at bay, to cherish his woman.

His woman. She'd always been his, he admitted finally, his heartbeat stepping up. Katherine would fight him over that later, would accuse him of being a possessive, chauvinistic male.

But she was his, and he grinned, anticipating the coming skirmish. When it came to fighting she had talent and he respected it. But when her causes were done he'd be waiting for her.

Katherine didn't want anyone in her private arenas, but she wasn't keeping him from her heart or her bed. Not after the savagery and the passion that had left him drained and stunned and ready for more.

She hadn't yet realized the commitment she'd made to him. Katherine had to be played, worn down and loved until she couldn't see straight or think. J.D. moved his head, taking a silky strand with his lips. He didn't intend to play fair, but he never had. And Katherine wasn't walking away free this time.

Her breath curled over his chest as she snuggled against him. She'd wanted him desperately. For now it was enough, but there would be more.

A lifetime of "mores," with Katherine fighting him every inch of the way. J.D. grinned, looking forward to the future and to fencing with Katherine.

At that moment she lay among the rumpled sheets like a well-fed, golden kitten. The Colorado sun had darkened her tawny skin, and her lashes lay softly on her flushed cheeks. Her mouth had a sensual look that hadn't been there before.

She shifted, drawing her left hand to her face to brush back a wayward strand of hair.

Sunlight entered the room, striking the Kelly diamond. A myriad of miniature explosions shot between Katherine and himself.

Whom had she loved so desperately last night? he wondered frantically. Had she loved Big Jim so deeply?

The diamond's brilliant facets cut at him like knife blades.

The pain of the past years rose to haunt him, and desperation filled his heart.

Easing himself away, J.D. stood and dressed quickly, aware that his hands were trembling. *Whom had she wanted so desperately in the night?*

He frowned as she turned over and snuggled deeper beneath the sheets. Suddenly he felt as though he needed a straight shot of whiskey.

Last night he'd opened himself to her. For a few hours he'd felt as though she'd given him a piece of her heart.

Katherine had needs; ones she couldn't yet admit.

He'd waited this long. He could wait some more, knowing that the two of them had come full circle.

But after this lovemaking there would be new rules, and he intended to keep her pretty back to the wall. She wasn't blaming him for making her decisions this time—*she'd* have to make the call.

Bending slowly, J.D. lifted the sheet to cover Katherine's bare shoulder. Letting his hand rest on the soft curve, he studied the angle of her jaw, the high, strong cheekbones and the sun-lightened hair.

"Kat, there are rules in this game of ours," he whispered. "I won't be used for the memory of a ghost. It's one on one now, sweet Angel."

Irish looked up from her coffee, surveying her sister's face; Katherine went on staring at her computer. "You haven't said a word all morning. You've been brooding more than a mother hen."

Katherine jotted down a note, then tapped her pencil on the desk. After their exhausting, fulfilling lovemaking three nights ago, J.D. had served her coffee in bed, then had settled down beside her to read his stock market report.

As he flipped through the pages she had wanted to throttle him. When he rose, still ignoring her, stretched and walked to the bathroom, anger shook her. She wanted to throw something at those well-shaped, pale buns, rippling with power. Padding across the thick carpeting, J.D. turned, just as she hefted a murder mystery from a bedside table. His eyebrows rose mockingly. "Ah...be nice, Kat. Are you in a snit because I didn't ask you to shower with me?" he asked mildly, watching her scramble out of bed—the scene of the crime. Unable to speak, she wrapped the sheet around her.

She'd wanted him again, had wanted sweet words and gentle touches. But from J.D.'s dark, contemplative expression, she knew he'd forced her to come after him. To ask for what she needed.

He wanted her soul, wanted to bend her to his will, but she wouldn't. So help her God, she wouldn't give him more.

He'd whistled in the shower and she'd hoped he'd drown as she dressed quickly and slammed out of his penthouse. From then on he'd been polite, surprising her with a tender kiss or lacing his fingers with hers. But he'd kept a distance.

Katherine glanced out the window, knowing perfectly well he'd set her needs in motion and was taunting her with them.

She hated waking up alone in the morning.

Exactly what right did J.D. have to avoid her? She'd worked herself into a state of exhaustion, trying to escape both that night and the recognition that J.D. would make her come after him. He was concerned about Travis entering Denver's day school program and about Irish's inn, and was acting as though Katherine was a pleasant acquaintance. Nettled, she curled her toes within her sneakers. "I'm just tired."

"Ha! Give me a break. You've been staring at J.D. like a cat waiting for a saucer of cow's cream."

Katherine glanced outside at J.D., who was working beneath the shade of an elegant maple tree. Shirtless, J.D. was using a pick to carefully extract the roots of a dead tree from Irish's bed of peonies.

The taste of his flesh lingered on her tongue.

She found herself studying the rippling muscles sheathed in sun-darkened skin, the untanned strip of flesh above his low jeans. The jeans tightened across his hips as he lifted the pick, slamming it into the earth. Katherine's palms grew damp, remembering the taut mounds of naked muscle.

Irish blithely dropped more words into the silence. "Something is eating at J.D., too. He's got that wary look. Like he could take something apart and isn't sure just what—that's why he's demolishing the flower garden."

"Stop matchmaking, Irish," Katherine ordered quietly, watching J.D. hand Travis the pick. Okay, she admitted she had needs. And irritating though it seemed, J.D. did satisfy them. But in spite of his neat little game of come-get-me, J.D. could wait until a glacier slid across the Sahara desert.

Retaining a grip on the pick handle, he showed the little boy how to chop at the hole. Katherine shifted her position, feeling odd, responding twinges. "I'm a little too old to start any fantasies now."

"Really? The spark is there. You two stir up storms when you're together. Something has changed between you."

Still drawn toward the window, Katherine's body ached. More than that, something inside her just wanted to walk into his arms and feel them wrap around her. That night with J.D. had left her as vulnerable as she had been at eighteen, the hunger beating within her. Then she awoke fully, realizing the depth of her feeling for this man she had hated for years.

Her fingers crushed the curtains. *Katherine, my love...*

She frowned, closing her eyes against the rising tears. People couldn't feed on dreams; they had to face up to reality.

"Pure whimsy," she whispered, her throat aching with tension. She wanted to take the night of exhausting, satisfying lovemaking and toss it into a file drawer marked To Be Opened In Another Century.

Katherine folded her arms around herself, allowing the curtain to fall between them as the years had done. J.D. had cut her too closely once. He could again, and she couldn't afford that now.

"I don't suppose you've seen this?" Irish thrust a gossip tabloid into Katherine's hand, pointing at a picture of J.D.'s dark head bent over her hand. The pose was both classical and romantic.

Katherine closed her eyes tight, trying to wipe out the image. The paper had appeared the morning after. And her office staff had responded with wall-to-wall leers when she'd told them she was returning to the inn.

While Katherine groaned, Irish giggled. "Now the whole world knows you've got a crush on him, Kat. Just look at the expression on your face." She tapped the paper.

Katherine swung toward her sister, anger starting to rise as she grabbed the paper in her fist. "I smell a very large rat."

"Now, Kat, wait a minute...."

Irish's voice faded as Katherine slipped through the open window, heading straight for J.D. Travis ran toward her, locking his arms around her legs, and Katherine paused on her journey to destruct MacLean. She crouched to hug the boy, kissing his cheek. "How are you?"

Travis pecked her cheek shyly, then grinned. "My grandpa likes you," he said brightly. "Me, too."

"Really?" Looking up at J.D., she said between her teeth, "It's a good thing Travis is here to save you."

She tossed down the paper near his boots and knew he was guilty when he didn't spare it a second glance.

Allowing his gaze to stroll slowly down her figure, J.D. whistled a low wolf call. "Maybe I don't want to be saved from a woman who can wear jeans like they were made for her."

Uncoiling herself, Katherine clenched her fists at her waist and glared at him. "I'm past the time you could sweet-talk me, J.D."

"I never tried. You're not the kind of woman who feeds on that sort of thing."

"Really? What do I feed on?" she demanded archly.

She wished she hadn't asked when his dark gaze went sliding to her mouth. She saw J.D. narrow his eyes, tilt his head and look down his nose at her. Stripping off his gloves, he shifted his feet, a move that tightened the worn jeans about his powerful thighs. He dusted a leaf from his shoulder, and his chest rippled beneath his sun-warmed flesh.

"You're in trouble, lady. So am I. It's just a matter of time," he said, quietly enough to rock the earth at her feet.

A distinct quiver ran the length of Katherine's legs. Fighting the heat that was curling within her, she kicked a rock with the toe of her sneaker.

J.D. followed the motion. "You're in a sweet mood this morning. I wonder why."

"You know why. You probably had a hand in pasting those pictures all over Denver." Katherine patted Travis's black head. "Irish is getting ready to paint the fence. Do you want to help her, Travis?"

When the little boy skipped away, J.D. bent to pick a delicate, pink wildflower. In a deft movement he tucked it into the crevice of her breasts beneath her blouse. He studied the effect while her anger grew. "Okay, spit it out, Kat," he said, still watching her.

She ripped the flower from her blouse, tossing it to the ground. "Why, damn you?"

When he reached out a finger to trace her lips, she jumped back, but the impression lingered after his hand had returned to his belt. "I want every man within touching distance of you to know you're mine."

"What?"

"We made love, Kat. Now there's no turning back. I don't want another man running interference for you, so I staked out my claim."

"What a dirty, rotten, low-life thing to do," she said when she could talk.

"I know." Then he grinned the devastating, rakish grin that sent her heart racing. "You can count on me."

He touched her cheek and she danced back, burned. Rubbing the spot, Katherine shivered in the afternoon sun.

His smile was not nice. "You don't like sharing a part of yourself, do you? I'm on to you now, lady. You've a need inside you as big as mine. But I'm going to give you time to put away your relics—including that damn ring. And then I'm calling the cards."

Slashing out her hand as if to stop him, Katherine trembled. "That night was something I want to forget. I have absolutely no intention of anything like that happening again."

"Toss it away with the dirty laundry? Or set the terms of when I touch you and you touch me? You won't be able to do that, Kat. Neither will I," he stated flatly. "Consider your ivory tower breached."

"Your confidence is overwhelming," she managed to declare through a suddenly tight throat. "Such arrogance. Perhaps we should have you bronzed."

He grinned. "Let's say the night with you called for extreme concentration."

Katherine's heart skipped a beat. He had no business making her want to throw herself into his strong arms and forget about everything but sun and fresh air.

Scowling at her thoughts, Katherine decided that J.D. was a well-packaged male illusion, one not to be trusted. When she took a step backward, J.D. stretched out a hand, wrapping his fingers around her upper arm and lowered his face to hers. She leaned back against the fingers that were caressing her nape.

"It's all in there, Kat," he said. "The passion and the loneliness. It won't go away."

Trying to draw away, Katherine placed one hand on his wrist, tugging at it. "My life is none of your business."

"Sure." His tone mocked her. "You gave me a night I'll never forget. Now everything about you is my business."

His fingers tightened, drawing her nearer him. "He's gone, Kat. You've mourned him, and now it's time to live."

He ran the pad of his thumb slowly down her cold cheek. "You don't like being reminded of how you lost control, do you?"

He gently eskimo-kissed her nose with his. Katherine had the urge to sink to the sun-warmed earth and twine herself about him.

His large hands skimmed down her back, caressing her hips beneath the tight jeans. Katherine closed her eyes, feeling as if she could melt into warm butter, her bones turning fluid. Tucking her within the cradle of his thighs, he moved sensuously against her. "Now this is therapy," he whispered, his mouth brushing her lips.

Astonished that she had unwillingly answered the slow rhythm of his thighs, Katherine groaned. "Ohh, I...I think that's enough."

"Mmm, for now, maybe. Just maybe." J.D. kissed her, leaving her wanting more, then he moved her away.

"It's nice to be needed, isn't it, Kat?" he asked quietly, studying her confused, flushed expression. "Men enjoy the feeling, too. Try that, Ms. Attorney-at-Law."

That evening at dinner, Katherine had the feeling of a mouse being stalked by a hungry tomcat. Or a defendant in a crime who knows that condemning evidence has just been discovered.

She also had to deal with the evening that stretched before her.

Beneath Irish's well-stocked dinner table Katherine smoothed her long, gypsy skirt with restless fingers. Taking them into his hand, J.D. laced her fingers with his. His stockinged foot slowly rubbed her shin. "I'm taking a truck to Creede, picking up lumber for Irish. How about coming, Kat?"

"No." He'd thrown out their so-called "relationship" for Irish to gloat over, staking his claim again. Yet the thought both irritated and pleased her.

Glaring at him, Katherine wanted to giggle and to lash out. Keeping her dignity was difficult while his toes crept around to tickle her ankle. She moved her leg away and his followed.

Freeing her hand, Katherine met his gaze. "No."

"Grandpa says the truck has a bed and everything," Travis offered, stabbing his broccoli.

"Don't be such a stick-in-the-mud, Kat," Irish added as Katherine and J.D. locked stares.

"She's afraid," J.D. drawled. "Something could happen to her if she stepped out of her safe courtrooms."

He stared at her across the ornate candle holder; the flames flickered between them, throwing shadows onto the dining-room wallpaper. "To all the tomorrows, Kat."

The next week—the first week of August—Katherine left Irish's world of brochures, lists and health menus to visit her office. She was quickly immersed in a heavy work load. Glancing at the mountains, she would allow herself a moment's mental vacation to wander through Irish's peony beds, then would grimly return to her cases.

On this particular day she crushed her notes into a ball after two hours and took a hasty look at the MacLean Building. Her thoughts had been with him rather than the schedules of the day, yet for years the law had been her solitary love. Katherine frowned and studied the vase filled with J.D.'s roses.

On her old diet of legalities and crusades she'd forgotten how to relax. Now she found herself savoring the fragrance rising from the petals of the red roses for the hundredth time that morning.

J.D.'s bold scrawl filled the florist's card: "Missing me?"

"Missing you?" she whispered, lifting a delicate bud to her cheek. "Impossible, J.D."

She brushed the bud across her lower lip, enjoying the sensuous softness. Kicking off her business pumps, Katherine propped her feet upon her desk.

"I've always liked a good challenge, J.D.," she murmured, closing her eyes as she lifted her hair away from her face, then let it trail slowly through her fingertips. Leaning back in her chair, Katherine allowed herself to think of him.

In recent days she'd moved into a spacious suite and had started tearing away at the enormous job of dissolving Big Jim's estate. Charities had received a large proportion and museums had appreciated his antiques, though she'd kept a few things to remember the time with him.

They'd been good years, but they weren't her future.

She toyed with the golden heart on her necklace. J.D. thought he knew the score.

Just maybe he didn't.

She wanted him every bit as off balance as he had kept her. Then, while he was trying to get his breath, she'd sweep Irish from his clutches.

Whatever relationship they had, she wanted Irish free from the backwash.

Katherine smiled, twisting a strand of hair around her finger. She'd show him she knew how to have fun. Ringing Mandy, she asked, "What is my schedule for next week?"

Tuesday morning J.D. stuffed her traveling bag into the sleeper cab and growled something that sounded like "Get in."

The eighteen-wheeler idled, waiting to surge onto the roads as J.D. leveled a hard stare at her. J.D. had topped his outfit of black T-shirt, jeans and boots with a ball cap that shaded his eyes. He ran his fingers through his sleek, damp hair, then gripped the gear lever. "You need a keeper. Don't you know it's dangerous to wait outside your apartment building?"

J.D. revved the engine and eased the semitruck onto the street in the early-morning light. The city was still sleeping. The truck roared along the interstate out of Denver like a primordial monster escaping to its bogs.

Running through a series of gears, J.D. glanced into the side mirror to check traffic. "What's your problem?" he asked curtly. Eyeing a passing truck in the mirror he muttered a curse. "Pour me coffee from that thermos."

J.D. had all the manners of a bear disturbed in his cave. Katherine couldn't resist teasing him. "Okay. Anything else you want, master?"

Flashing a blank stare at her, J.D. grumbled something about smart-mouthed, sassy women in the morning.

Obviously, J.D. needed his coffee. "Bad night, hon?" she questioned innocently, thoroughly enjoying the moment. In the past she'd seen him angry or amused, but this grumpy, ill-shaven man of the morning was something new and completely intrigued her.

He glanced at her. "More guppies. All night. I filled out papers for Travis's preschool and listened to him talk about how wonderful you are."

"Oh, my. We did miss our sleep," she crooned sympathetically, pouring coffee for both of them and settling back to enjoy the pink dawn.

J.D. glared at her, looking as ominous as a Ute chief on the warpath. "So I'm human," he admitted darkly as they passed a soaring stand of pines.

"Playing Superman is challenging." Smothering a smile, Katherine surveyed the mountainous scenery ahead. J. D. MacLean, tough trucking mogul, sleepless and grumpy because he'd wanted his grandson to experience the birth of guppies.

Scowling at her, J.D. stepped on the gas to gather speed for a small rise. "Are you trying to start something?"

"Oh, no, sir."

"Cut it out."

Katherine grinned, feeling great. "Gotcha. Would you like another cup of coffee?"

Finding her face in the cab's mirror he stared at her for a moment. "No, I'd rather have you slide over here."

In the silvery rectangle Katherine found herself drowning in J.D.'s steady gaze.

She had to know. "Why?"

"I've missed you," he returned simply. Taking her hand, he lifted it to his lips.

His warm tongue slid along her soft, inner palm. J.D. rubbed her hand against his hard thigh, watching her in the mirror all the while. "I could pull over."

Katherine flushed instantly and looked away. Their intimacy was too new, too fragile—

He kissed her hot cheek. "It's okay, Kat. I'm winded, too. Why don't you just settle back and enjoy the drive?"

For the rest of the day Katherine discovered that J.D. could sing with any of his tapes from country and western to rock and roll. The tight strings within her loosened as the truck swept past the rugged scenery.

In the late afternoon she yawned and J.D. nudged her with his shoulder. "We're almost to a diner. Lean on me." The request was almost a question.

"I'm so tired," she said, resting her head against his shoulder.

"You've been running too hard. I've been there."

It was dusk when J.D. pulled the truck into the parking space of a café with a neon light proclaiming that this was Sam's Place.

The small bar cum restaurant was filled with truckers and locals. While they finished platters of steak and potatoes, the owner and cook planted his ample body at their table. "Howdy, J.D. Haven't seen you in a spell. This your old lady?" he asked around a well-chewed toothpick. His voice sounded like steam forcing itself out of rusty pipes. "Ain't much meat there, boy."

"You know what they say about dynamite."

Sam chuckled. "Comes in small packages." He stuck out his meaty hand, ready to shake Katherine's. "So you're the fox who trapped the old lonesome wolf, huh? I'll bet that took some wrangling."

Wanting to give J.D. a dose of his own medicine, Katherine patted his broad shoulder. "He was a pushover."

"I know better, lady. J.D.'s been running from hungry women for years," Sam told her when he stopped laughing.

Apparently J.D. had some secrets he wanted to keep buried. "Really?" she asked, enjoying J.D.'s menacing scowl at Sam.

"Uh-huh. Hey, Doris, take another pitcher to table two on the house," he called to the waitress. "They just got married."

Sam chewed his toothpick thoughtfully. "Kids just got married—don't have a pot to their name, too young, and don't have enough sense to know better," he explained roughly. "I always thought J.D. here was some kinda love victim," he offered, clapping J.D. on the shoulder.

"Sam, we need to be shoving off," J.D. told him.

He looked distinctly uncomfortable, Katherine decided. The look suited him, she thought, and settled down to enjoy Sam's breathy dialogue. "I'd love to hear about it."

Sam shoved back his chair and surged to his feet, smoothing the apron that covered his belly. "Nah. How 'bout singing a song for old Sam, J.D.?" he asked, then bent to confide to Katherine, "Used to haul his kid in here. Sang for her...." He shook his head. "Sorry, J.D. So's how about a song? I still got that old guitar."

Recognizing the grief that was coursing through J.D.'s dark, brooding expression, Katherine placed one hand on his.

Meeting her eyes, J.D. agreed softly without looking at Sam. "Don't blame me if your customers complain, Sam."

Leaning against the bar, J.D. slowly took up the guitar, fingering it in silence. Drawing it to himself like a lover, he played a delicate version of "Greensleeves." The crowd grew quiet as the soft melody curled about the diner. Then, bracing his boot upon a chair, he strummed a flamenco, its intensity and heat marked in his frown of concentration.

The music soared, plunged, ensnared Katherine in its passionate mist. J.D.'s lean fingers traveled quickly across the taut strings, the tempo catching her heartbeat.

Lifting her eyes, she found him staring hungrily at her. A sleek strand of hair crossed his forehead, moving with the rhythm of his music. Beneath his brows, J.D.'s eyes seared her own, his lips pressed tightly together, his forehead damp.

In that instant Katherine found herself caught up in the intensity of her own emotions. The hard angles of his face and body seemed so isolated, so in need of love—

Love? Katherine swallowed quickly, her hands clenched tightly together as he began to sing "Love Me Tender."

She could feel his music reach into her, asking her to step into the future. Acting on feminine instincts she hadn't trusted in eons, Katherine rose and stood beside him.

The moment hovered between them; the tenderness in J.D.'s expression soothed her wounds. She placed a hand on his bare arm.

The muscles rippled beneath her touch as his hands flowed over the guitar. Within herself the life pulse throbbed slowly, warmly.

She needed him. Needed to take and to give.

When the music faded, the crowd was silent, waiting for more.

Beside her Sam sniffed and wiped his eyes. "Haven't heard him play like that in years. Straight out of his heart. The songs would tear your gut out. Sounded like an old lonesome timber wolf crying for his mate."

"It was rough back then," J.D. said softly, looking into Katherine's eyes. "No money, broken-down trucks, Daisy needing me. Sam helped by letting me sing here when we came through, for a few dollars and enough free food to help us get by."

"When *we* came through?" Katherine asked.

"I took Daisy with me every chance I could."

Sam shook his head. "Rough times."

"Times are changing," J.D. murmured, drawing Katherine to him for a lingering, sweet kiss.

Ten

The first week of September came and Katherine, in her office, listened to Travis chattering happily away at the other end of the line. Secure in the love that surrounded him, Travis bore the trademark of MacLean Devastation, Inc. Appealing, loving and more than a handful, he was busy marketing his guppies to friends at his preschool. Recently, he told her, he had lugged home an extremely pregnant cat as payment. "I love you," he ended cheerfully and she returned the sentiment, meaning it. Replacing the receiver, she thought how much they had all changed.

Once again red roses decorated her desk. J.D. had sent them, and she found herself remembering again the sound of the rain beating against the truck cab, the steamy hungers racing within.

"This is a dream," she had whispered, draped drowsily across him, his hand stroking her damp neck.

"No, it's reality," he had murmured against her throat.

She had held him tightly then, frightened for the future. "Oh, J.D. What are we going to do?"

His arm had gathered her closer, the possession making her safe. "Ride it out."

She had lifted her head, appraising his mood in the shadows as rain coursed down the truck windows. With new confidence she'd trailed her fingers across his mouth, pleasured as he kissed them. "I like having things my way."

"So do I," he had responded, filling her with his passion.

Now Katherine touched the roses on her desk.

Courting her before the entire city of Denver, J.D. carefully paced his pursuit. Outings with Travis were a favorite, or candlelight dinners in the best restaurants and plays. He'd flown her to Irish's for two weekends, but preparations for the grand opening had kept them all busy.

On business days his ten o'clock evening call had kept her awake for hours. His voice had the sound of a lover waiting. . . .

Katherine impatiently pushed aside a large stack of paper. Taking the corner of the battered, crayon poster, she held it up, studying Travis's latest artistic effort. In vivid colors he'd caught the September hues of the mountains—orange aspen leaves splashed with the blues and greens of firs and pines.

A large, smiling face on a woman depicted Irish, who was both happy and frantic as plans developed for her early October "Whindig," a weekend charity affair. Bus tours would carry Denver socialites down to the remodeled inn and into Irish's waiting, caring hands.

Katherine smiled at the stick man and woman labeled "Kat" and "Grandpa." Between the two MacLean males she'd been neglecting her causes. Travis called her daily and had adjusted to his new preschool class. On occasions when J.D. was out of town on business, the youngster had made a shambles of her spacious apartment. Travis, a miniature

J.D., knew exactly how to ensnare her for a video game or a lazy afternoon of coloring books.

For a time Katherine had suspected J.D. of planting Travis in her heart. Bathed and drowsy, the little boy could snuggle against her in a way that destroyed her defenses—and was easily satisfied with fudge brownies.

But J.D. wanted everything.

Katherine lifted a long-stemmed bud from the bouquet, trailing it dreamily along her cheek. J.D.'s late-night phone calls were calculated to torment her, the raspy, male voice sending images of the night they'd spent in the truck.

He knew how to catch her on the raw, too. Like leaving her well-kissed and aching for him. They were fencing; she knew it.

Shrugging aside the sensual forays, she acknowledged that J.D. was an interesting companion. One to explore.

On the subject of Irish's financial partnership with him they had come to a Mexican standoff, neither fighter giving an inch. But then Irish was on her own, Katherine had decided lately. Her baby sister would have to find her own ten-o'clock caller.

Placing the rose on the desk, Katherine pinpointed the MacLean building beyond her window. J.D. was playing games. She didn't like the secret amusement in his black eyes—not a bit. She'd twisted her wedding ring, a new habit, and smiled. Until now she'd allowed him the advantage as he followed his male courtship rites.

She flipped open the file on her latest case. A young divorcée with three children had been sexually harassed in her workplace. Katherine methodically sifted the details, taking notes for her summation the next day. The woman was exotically beautiful, with a voluptuous figure that drew men's eyes. She was also an intelligent wage earner and a dedicated mother, pressured by male executives to "play ball."

Taking just a moment from her preparation, Katherine glanced at her ring. She'd worn it so long out of love, clinging to her husband's memory. He'd been her mentor, her friend, encouraging her to "take on the evil hordes."

As she moved her finger, the ring seemed cold now, the memories fading. "I think, Big Jim, that you and I are going to have a talk."

Wouldn't have it an other way, honey, she could almost hear him saying. *Give him hell, girl. Go for it.*

At precisely nine-thirty that evening Katherine lay back on her couch and reached for the telephone. She lifted her left hand and studied the now ringless finger for a moment. "Time to go on, Big Jim," she whispered.

Then she dialed J.D.'s home number. His answer was abrupt. "MacLean here."

Katherine stretched one pajama-clad leg and wriggled her red-hot tinted toes. She studied the shade, enjoying the slightly "sinful" whim of the evening and anticipating the conversation. "Katherine here."

"What's wrong?" He rapped out the question, the genuine concern in his tone almost making her ashamed of her caper.

"Nothing." She ran her bare insole along the arm of her cream velvet couch.

"Why are you calling, Kat? Are you sure nothing's wrong?"

Twisting her finger around a strand of hair, Katherine let herself enjoy the mental picture of J.D. running his hand through *his* hair. It was a gesture of distraction usually accompanied by a scowl that drew his black eyebrows together. "What are you doing?"

He inhaled roughly, impatiently. "Paperwork. We're setting up a new schedule for a cross-country run and faster loading procedures. Buying a fleet of trucks in the morning," he added as an afterthought, as though he were purchasing vanilla cream puffs.

"Mmm." Katherine turned onto her stomach. J.D. had deliberately paced his calls to entice her. She could surely do the same. Asking a series of questions yielded an appropriate set of rather gruff answers. "Am I keeping you from something?" she asked pleasantly.

"Kat, I'm coming over there if you don't tell me why you called."

Settling back on the tasseled pillows, she glanced again at her bare finger. She was stronger now; she had recognized that she needed more than causes.

Tormenting J.D. was a good starter.

"But J.D., I'm ready for bed." Licking her upper lip, Katherine decided she liked jumping ahead of J.D.; it made him so nicely... edgy.

There was a distinct pause at the other end of the line. He laughed, the deep sound intimate and rawly male. "Is that my first invitation to enter the Kelly inner sanctum?"

"You've been here before." Katherine rubbed her cheek against the velvet, remembering the heavy thud of his heart.

"Uh-huh. To deliver and pick up Travis. What are you doing, Kat? Playing beck and call?"

Closing her eyes, Katherine allowed herself to fall into her own game. Flirting with J.D. was a pastime she could enjoy night after night. Lowering her voice to a husky tone of invitation, she answered with a smile, "There's just little old me in this big apartment."

Inhaling sharply, J.D. cleared his throat. "Something is wrong. Ring the doorman and tell him to let me in, Kat."

Crossing her fingers, Katherine threw in the coup de grace. "Not tonight. I'm ending a tough case first thing in the morning." She paused for just the right amount of time, then added, "I still have to try on those costumes Irish wants me to model at the Whindig."

"What costumes?" She liked the distinctly proprietary tone of his voice.

"Oh, you know, costumes from the madame's business era. They're a little bit low on my—"

"Those scraps are indecent. There's not enough material to cover your—" he paused "—chest or that sweet little fanny. I won't have you parading around in anything that shows so much skin."

"You liked that scrap," she pointed out, smiling at her success. "Besides, you haven't got anything to say about it."

"Kat," he breathed heavily, impatiently. "Think twice about this."

"Do you really think my fanny is nice?" she asked innocently, then listened to an explosion of male outrage about women being kept on leashes. Actually she knew he didn't feel that way at all—about women in general. J.D. graded women as equals, and remembering his own hard times had recently instituted a top-class, twenty-four-hour-day-care center for his employees. Any woman in his company was fully protected from discrimination, encouraged to take training programs with men and advance at an equal pace.

"It will be all right, honey," she soothed in sugar-coated tones when he stopped for a breath. "Good night. Sweet dreams."

Hugging herself, Katherine leaned back her head and grinned, kicking her heels on the upholstery. The childish gesture of excitement felt wonderful, so she indulged herself again.

At three o'clock the next day Katherine hugged her client, after winning the case. While the crowd moved by her table, she sorted papers into her briefcase, sitting quietly for a moment in the oak chair.

The hairs at the nape of her neck rose slightly, J.D.'s clean scent swirled around her and she felt his large hand settle on the jacket of her business suit. "Hi," she said simply, running her fingers across the worn briefcase. "We won."

His thumb brushed her cheek lightly. "Rough one, huh?"

"Had to fight like hell."

He fitted his palm to the back of her neck and Katherine found herself leaning against his strength. Somehow her hand found its way to his wrist, the rough texture familiar and safe.

Lifting her face, Katherine looked at J.D. In a navy-blue suit, he was every inch the successful businessman. But now a tenderness lurked in his black eyes, a certain softening curved his lips. The autumn wind had caught his sleek hair, tousling it. The strand she'd so often seen crossed his forehead, softening the lines.

Katherine reached to smooth back that errant, blue-black strand.

The gesture was simple—a possessive, caring sign from a woman who cared for a man.

Testing the emotion as he stood perfectly still, she straightened his blue- and maroon-striped tie. Running her fingers across his collar, she adjusted it meticulously.

"What's going on in there, Counselor?" he asked roughly, warily as he tapped her forehead.

Katherine stood on tiptoe and brought life into the sterility of the empty courtroom as she lightly kissed his cheek. "I think you need someone to keep you in line, J.D."

"This case must have taken a lot out of you," he observed a little unevenly, tracing her features with concerned eyes.

Inhaling sharply, he cupped her elbow in a courtly gesture. Katherine smiled, watching his frown deepen. Gently she slipped her fingers into the safe warmth of his free hand.

Katherine discovered she liked walking down the courthouse halls beside J.D. Shortening his stride to hers, he moved beside her like someone who would always be there. The strength of his hand sheathed her own, the heat of his body was comforting.

She liked stepping into the crisp, autumn air with him.

With a hard look at her, J.D. muttered, "Kat, you look damned tired. You're going home."

Riding her new discoveries, Katherine meekly agreed, "That would be nice."

His hesitation was rewarding. "You're actually accepting my suggestion. This must be a milestone." The wind sweeping her hair across her face, Katherine allowed J.D. to tuck her into her Jeep with a strict order to follow his Range Rover.

A half hour later in her suite, J.D. eased her onto her bed, taking off her pumps. Sitting on the edge of the bed, he rubbed her arches, concentrating on the gentle task. He wrapped his hand around her slender ankle, and Katherine settled back on the satin pillows. She intended to enjoy having J.D. hover around her like a mother hen. "Don't you have something important to do?"

"Not a thing. Closed a deal for a fleet of new trucks this morning, and Travis is staying overnight with a friend. They've decided to raise gerbils.... I needed the rest. Your call kept me awake all night."

Running a finger across her toes, he lifted a brow—the one with the scar soaring through it. "Red polish? A little on the wild side for angels, isn't it?"

"Mmm." She noted that his voice no longer held sarcasm when he called her Angel. When he called her "his angel," she almost went limp with emotion.

Wriggling her toes, she enjoyed J.D. capturing them gently, sliding his fingers around each one. The gesture was erotic. Fascinating. And entirely improper for a leading businessman. "Do you have a foot fetish?" she asked, wanting him to hold her.

His hands fell still. "I have a fetish for everything about you. Your toes, however, are highly excitable, and you know it. Do you want to tell me anything about the case today?"

Sharing her life wasn't something that came easily, she decided slowly as his thumbs massaged her insoles. She had missed the feeling, and now the need to indulge herself was overwhelming.

She'd been missing so much. Exploring both J.D. and her own emotions was a case she had to build carefully. "Prejudices against women in the business world grate."

Wriggling his eyebrows lewdly, J.D. whispered a W. C. Fields aside: "Ah, the old bosoms versus brains scam."

She giggled helplessly, feeling the tension ease out of her. "Something like that."

"Keep it up, Blondie," he continued, mimicking the comic. "And you'll have to explain the floozy paint."

The polish matched an entire set of new, lacy lingerie. But J.D. would have to discover that fact on his own. The anticipation was delicious. He needed surprises to keep him on edge. Or from taking complete control.

She was tired, she realized as J.D. sat there, holding her hand and looking like a sexy, appealing angel of mercy. "What's the protocol now?" he asked, rubbing her calves.

"Hot tea and a long nap." Closing her eyes, Katherine felt him lift his weight from the bed. Normally she'd return to her office and work on another case into the night. But not right now. She wanted to enjoy J.D. taking charge.

She awoke hours later to find her clothing loosened and a cold cup of tea beside her bed. J.D., his shirt opened and shoes off, snored pleasantly beside her.

Listening quietly, Katherine probed her feelings. The sound was comforting. Nice. Like the wind swishing through mountain pines. Sliding her hand across his bare chest, Katherine played with the dark hair that covered it. The texture was familiar, endearing. Something she could nestle into.

Smiling in the darkness, Katherine placed her cheek on his shoulder.

J.D. did have his pluses.

J.D. sat in the back of the courtroom and observed Katherine coolly stalking a reluctant witness in a fraudulent housing project. The September sunshine flowed through the tall, elegant windows of the courtroom, lighting her hair.

His fingers moved slightly as he mentally tested the silky strands and their varying shades of silver and dark gold. The two of them had settled for an emotional, Mexican stand-off that could turn into heaven or hell at any moment.

Katherine tapped the witness railing. She was closing in on the witness, getting ready to nail the man to his lies— Her navy business suit and pumps covered a body that had curled to him like a kitten in the truck, J.D. recalled.

In her private arena, the courtroom, Kat was dangerous. J.D.'s hard mouth tightened, his attention locked on the woman who dominated the room, her voice quiet and deadly.

Could this be the same person who had wiped away Travis's tears last night?

Rubbing his hand down his taut thigh, J.D. allowed himself a deep frown. He traced the shape of the small ring box in his slacks pocket.

Not accepting anything from him, Katherine had him at knife point. Maybe she always had. But she wasn't wearing the Kelly brand, and that had to mean something.

Katherine swept across the spacious courtroom. The brilliant sunlight shone in through a tall window, catching the dark and light strands of her hair. She had yet to indicate a commitment, he thought. Their tenuous relationship was laced with late-night calls and sweet, lingering kisses that frustrated the hell out of him.

Katherine suddenly slashed at the witness, causing the fat, balding man to blanch. Her eyes would be almost black now, the aspen-colored flecks obliterated by raw fury. Meticulous, yet daring, she closed in on the man, catching him in a lie that clinched the case.

For a tense moment Katherine looked at the man as though she were blowing smoke off the barrel of her six-gun, a job well-done. When she lifted her left hand to run it through her hair, J.D. wanted her finger circled with his own ring, a specially designed array of gold and smoky topaz.

But Katherine was taking her time, driving him mad. Choosing her place and time for the final draw. He couldn't demand more than she would give.

Keeping herself on a taut line, Katherine still had her secrets. J.D. suspected that one of them was the depth of her emotions. She was always in control; but when she began to feel that edge slipping, she got a wild-eyed, panicked look.

When she turned, her gaze seeking him, J.D. felt the full blast of her triumph. Sharing it silently with him, Katherine smiled slowly.

Then the tip of her tongue slid out to trail across her upper lip, and every thought J.D. possessed went slithering out the courtroom door.

Katherine had developed an odd sense of humor, he decided.

October blew in with a gust of Arctic air and a skift of early snow. The inn was filled with the laughter of Denver socialites.

On opening night Abagail's lights burned brightly, the chandeliers and lamps properly converted to electricity. The guests crowded into the small bedrooms with the air of explorers discovering a new world.

Dressed in clothing of the madame's era, laughing patrons crowded into the parlor and ballroom combination. Irish handed Katherine a tray of crystal glasses filled with the inn's special mineral water. Dressed in a heavy satin dress with a plunging bodice, Irish grinned. "Ever since J.D. saw you wearing the madame's outfit and that Chinese wrapper, he's been acting like a bear with a sore paw. He's muttering things about your costume. Like how indecent it is.

He's definitely one unhappy dude. Especially when you laugh."

Irish glanced at the miniature stage, where a miniplay about the madame would be presented, and grinned again. "Just after the play the lights will flicker—don't you think that's a nice touch?"

"I haven't seen J.D. for two weeks." Katherine ignored her sister's attempts to revive the madame, thinking of J.D.'s whimsical male logic. He too was playing games, holing up in his businesses and with his grandson.

She wanted to see him, and now that they were in the same room together, he was suddenly acting like—a lover with rights.

Irish adjusted the red plume that soared from Katherine's elaborate curls. "I know it's silly, Kat. But there's this little thing called male pride. It's up to us women to see that it remains intact. All it costs is a little petting and pampering. When it comes right down to it, he's just an overgrown Travis. I wish Travis were here."

"Travis is sweet and lovable. His grandmother probably questions that right now, though Travis is probably enjoying ruling her." Katherine's eyes skimmed J.D.'s tall body, looming behind a giant, potted fern. Dressed in gambler's black, he drew appreciative, feminine stares. When his gaze locked with Katherine's, she felt the impact low in her stomach. Now J.D. appeared nothing like the considerate companion he had been in Denver.

"He looks quite...savage," Katherine found herself saying. "He's not all that tough, you know. I can take him on with one hand tied behind my back."

She just might have to go after him, she thought. Seduce him and show him that his place was next to her.

Irish let out a peal of laughter, startling the guests nearby. "If you think that, good luck. J.D. can be nudged, pampered and petted into a direction, but I have yet to see him ruled. Besides, didn't you once think he had a heart of concrete?''

Katherine smoothed the long sausage curl that covered her nape. "Well, I could change my mind. He's doing some nice work in rehab and centers for abused women and children. He's working with a group that uses volunteer professionals to train and help people with their problems."

Irish stared at her as if she had stepped into an alien world. "I knew that all along."

"It isn't common knowledge. J.D. keeps a pretty tight lid on his activities. Without investigating I wouldn't have known. And he's a pushover where Travis is concerned. He loves him."

"Kat, he's dying for you. Watching you two together is like watching Clark Gable and Vivien Leigh in *Gone with the Wind*. You're nothing at all like you were before this summer. You're healthier. You even laugh now—well, not all that much."

Fluttering the tasseled fan before her face, Katherine agreed. "I'd been running too hard, then. Angry, perhaps with you—"

"With me?" Irish smiled automatically at a balding patron, then turned back to Katherine. "Kat, that doesn't sound like you."

Katherine shrugged, remembering. "I was too tired, running on sheer willpower. You weren't letting me have my usual way, Irish. And with J.D. lurking around, I had no idea what would happen. I began realizing that somewhere along the way I'd let my life rule me, not the other way around. For a person who likes to feel she's in control, the realization was devastating. When I started thinking about J.D. and you—"

"You're kidding!" Irish let out a peal of giggles, briefly drawing the crowd's attention. "J.D. is like a brother to me."

Katherine arched her brows. "I didn't know that at the time. He's always been attractive to women. To him you could have been…interesting. And I knew he was using you to antagonize me."

Irish shrugged. "If it's confession time, maybe I'd better admit I set this whole thing up. You were so perfect for each other. Mmm, maybe I'll start a matchmaking service."

"Enough. You've got too many ideas now. I sorted the grisly details some time ago. You had a number of options for financial help, and the way you were pushing J.D.'s selling points, your plot was obvious."

"Really? I'll have to be more subtle next time. Anyway, I knew you'd jump into the spaghetti noodles if I was in danger. So I just used myself as bait. You always were short on the fun side. Much too serious, nagging at details and examining everything for criminal elements—honestly!"

Katherine shot a nervous glance at J.D., who had stopped to talk to a gorgeous blonde with tousled hair and vacant, blue eyes. "I am fun," she muttered stiffly. "You make me sound like some hag running around in legal robes, searching for ulterior motives while I control everything in sight—like a queen bee," she added tightly.

Crossing her arms, Irish nodded slowly. "You're too cautious."

"I play tennis and I've put up with your tarot fortune-telling cards. Somewhere in there I must have a sense of humor."

"It's just that you hold everything in." Irish waved to a plump woman in a tight, cobalt-blue gown. "Mrs. Fredrich Fremont. If she likes us, we're in. I'm going to put her on a veggie diet the first thing."

But Katherine was watching the blonde, who was twining her arms around J.D.'s lean middle. He laughed, and Katherine scowled as the generous breasts melded to him. Did *he* see her as a controlling hag in legal robes? "Fun," she repeated under her breath. "I'll show both of you."

Tapping her sister's shoulder briskly, Irish said, "Go for it, champ."

Katherine narrowed her sights on J.D., who was chuckling at something the blonde had said. Recognizing a slice of jealousy, she waited for it to die. Was that how J.D. had felt when she married years ago?

The realization sent her reeling as though from a physical blow. He'd been hurt, trying to do what was best and ignoring his own needs back then. How he must have ached to see her with Big Jim. She closed her eyes, willing the tears back.

In his place would she have survived?

In his place she would have taken the same option for revenge.

Katherine opened her eyes just as the sexy, tall Venus moved against J.D. It was the right thing to do if the woman wanted her wrists broken, Katherine thought darkly.

The blonde's hands skimmed J.D.'s white, ruffled shirt, and Katherine found herself taking an involuntary step toward them. It was pure jealousy, something she couldn't control.

Her nails bit into her palms. If those pale hands slipped any lower on J.D.'s backside, Katherine would put her red-lacquered nails to use.

Sipping her mineral water, Katherine admitted having a few, uncontrollable, pagan needs. Especially when the woman's hands moved over J.D.'s jaw. That jaw was hers. Private territory. Katherine tapped her nails on the sleeve of her Chinese silk wrapper.

Without another thought she marched up to him. "I want to see you in my office, right now."

When he arched an eyebrow, mocking her, she corrected her mistake. "In the side parlor."

The potted palms swayed as she entered the room; the door closed quietly behind J.D. The lock clicked shut as she turned on him and crossed her arms. "Having fun, are we?" she asked between her teeth.

"I'm managing. How about you?" he asked as tightly.

"Your friend Evan has his hands all over you."

"Evan?" Watching J.D., she had barely acknowledged Evan's conversation, and he had moved away.

J.D.'s black eyes flashed with anger. Then his gaze strolled slowly down her costume, lingering on the slender curves of pale thighs covered by black fishnet stockings. "Honey, dressed like that you're fatal. Any man would think about making love to you. I'll probably be thinking about making love to you when I'm a hundred. By the way, I thought I told you not to wear that getup."

Drumming her forefinger on J.D's hard chest, Katherine spoke carefully. "You haven't been around to say anything. Much less dish out macho orders."

J.D. wrapped a hand around the nape of her neck, tightening his jaw. "I've been waiting for you to run through your paces, fitting me into your life. I don't suppose you missed me," he ground out accusingly.

"For what? Someone to tell me what I need?" Even in her anger she knew J.D. would hold firm, matching her best shots. It was a good feeling. He was a man to weather the worst of storms, in anger and in the good times.

She could level with him and that was a plus. He'd thrown some punches, but she had few of her own. "You seemed to need a certain blonde a few moments ago. Her hands were all over you."

His face went blank. "Jasmine?"

"Yes, J.D., dear. Jasmine with the overflowing bosoms and hot, lusting sequins." Somewhere in the functioning, normal part of her brain, Katherine realized she'd never felt this way before. Rage, jealousy, and the need to declare to the world that J.D. was hers.

He needed a big stamp across his forehead that read Taken. Find Another.

Oh, it was silly and primitive, of course. Just as primitive as the need to tear off his clothes and make him hers, binding him to her with all the little "I do's."

She shivered a little, realizing the depth of her emotions as J.D.'s dark frown became a sensual grin. Running a finger down her throat, he asked, "Are we experiencing a little flurry of jealousy, Katherine, dear?"

"Of course not," she snapped, too quickly. Then, as his fingertips traced the edge of her low bodice, she realized that the power play had moved to another level. But then, any time she had discussions with J.D., it was like stepping through quicksand.

There just had to be a happy medium.

"Your bosom is just fine, Kat," he rasped, bending to kiss her earlobe. "As bosoms go, it's class A."

The room was suddenly very close, the oxygen supply extremely limited as J.D. stepped nearer. She swallowed the tight wad of tension lodged in her throat, excitement skimming over her suddenly hot flesh.

"I really don't want to get into this now," she managed to say as his mouth brushed hers and warning bells started to clang. "Jasmine could be waiting for you."

He chuckled; it was a warm, rich, masculine sound that set her nerves dancing. "When can we discuss our mutual policies?" he pressed, the heat growing between them as he touched the softness of her hair.

"I think we should sort out our problems in a logical way." She inhaled as his breath swirled about her ear. His teeth tugged at the eardrop and she grew weak.

"Mmm. Logical," he repeated in a very deep tone, one that weakened her legs.

"As soon as we can transfer the partnership papers from you to me," she stated quickly, feeling her reasoning abilities beginning to fade.

J.D. tensed; he was breathing heavily now. After a moment he rasped pleasantly against her ear, "Do you know how damned bullheaded and unromantic you are, Katherine, my love?''

Midnight seemed the perfect time to call in Katherine's ex-client—a lady cat burglar. New locks had been installed in the madame's private retreat, and Katherine wanted to pick them.

"No fun, and not romantic, am I?" she muttered after receiving the expert's advice. Drawing the red plume across her chest, Katherine turned in front of the full-length, oval mirror. "Bullheaded and unromantic," she repeated darkly, tugging at her full-length cape. She adjusted the blood-red satin folds about her shoulders and lifted the hood to cover her hair.

A hunter's moon lighted the stained glass window. A gust of wind brought a flurry of leaves pattering against the pane.

Taking her time, Katherine lifted a small notepad and began checking off the list, probing the contents of a large basket. "Scented candles. Food for a day. Cassettes with romantic music. A few of the madame's costumes... check."

Katherine tapped the wicker basket's handle with her fingertips, frowning as she watched the smoke rise from the cottage's rock chimney. "The man needs to be taught a few lessons...."

Watching the small cottage grow dark, Katherine narrowed her eyes. Oh, she craved him, of course. The restlessness in her body was evidence enough. He was guilty of making her feel the need to hold and be held.

She wanted the deep whispers of the night and the silent understanding after a bad case. She needed the tea growing cold beside her bed and the man snoring softly as he lay stretched beside her.

J.D. was tough; but so was she. She needed that: someone to stand his ground.

And she needed to be needed. Because J.D. did need her, whether he knew it or not. To tame him just a little, so that he wouldn't end his days as a crusty old bachelor. To adjust his tie and worry over him.

To love him into eternity.

Hugging the thought to her, Katherine felt warm inside. Snugly. And, most of all, needed.

Katherine waited, examining her feelings for J.D. She'd hated him once for making a crucial decision for her. He'd wanted the best for her and been badly hurt in the process.

She could level with him and she could love him. The rest would come.

But she could not tolerate the label "unromantic."

"I really botched it," J.D. muttered, crouching to stare at the flames. "Typical of my less than suave tactics."

The Rocky Mountain night was cold, kept at bay by the fire in the madame's sumptuous fireplace. In the multiple mirrors J.D. found himself dressed in black briefs and very much alone in the dark.

He wanted her, damn it. Every stubborn, willful inch.

He'd hated her for years, had wrapped himself in the agony of not knowing why she had married Big Jim. Pain had made her lash out at him, he knew now, waving her husband in front of him.

Glancing into the moonlit night, J.D. traced the trails that zigzagged up the mountain. His own life had been like that: turning, twisting, but always headed in one direction—toward Katherine.

He'd deliberately stayed away from her for two weeks, testing her. Katherine had the tendency to be too smug. Every once in a while he'd have to remember that and rattle her. Katherine was always at her best when she was scrambling for control. Or *out* of control, meeting him in an ultimate burst of sensual pleasure. Or sated and feminine in his arms.

Taking a deep breath, J.D. lay back on his water bed to study the flames. So he needed to take care of her. But when she started flowing into him, her musky scent tantalizing him as they blended into one, J.D. knew he always stopped thinking.

He stroked the satin comforter with his thumb. For years he'd tried getting her out of his system with work and with other women. But she'd been burned into his blood, his soul, and there she would stay.

A pine knot caught fire, shooting out a burst of tiny sparks. *But Katherine was there to stay.*

A shadow passed across the window and he heard the door rattle. J.D. got up to check things out.

Eleven

———

Get in here before you catch your death of cold, woman!"
J.D. ordered, wrapping his fist in Katherine's satin cape. In
a second he had hauled her into the warm room and closed
the door. "What in hell are you doing, Kat?"

She shivered, realizing exactly how freezing the Rocky
Mountain winds could be on naked flesh. Glaring at J.D.'s
scowl, she thought how like him it was to spoil a romantic
moment. One she had planned. Her glance flashed uneasily down J.D.'s lean body. The black briefs, on the other
hand, were definitely romantic. Let him scowl, she decided, placing her basket on a small table and drawing the
cape closer. When she pushed back the cape's hood, her
fingers trembled slightly.

She didn't want him to see how nervous she was, coming
to him this way—taking the first step and offering herself.
He'd been taking pieces of her all along, and now she
wanted to set the terms in her own way.

"What's with the Little Red Riding Hood caper, Kat?"
His deep, humorous drawl warmed her like a lover's hands.
"Or are you really Abagail?"

"If you had given me just a moment longer, I could have
picked the lock, J.D. I know how." She was edgy, even defensive. He did that to her.

Katherine straightened her shoulders. The night would be
romantic and fun, she'd promised herself. She'd throw his
remarks right back into his devastatingly appealing, sexily
grinning face.

Taking a deep, steadying breath, she whipped off her
cape—and revealed the madame's scanty nightie, appropriately bedecked with sequins and tassels. Running her
hands through her hair, Katherine watched J.D.'s eyes go
dark, glittering in the light of the fire.

She responded to him without missing a beat and
promptly stored her night of romance and fun in the Tomorrow bin. "I missed you," she whispered quietly and
meant it.

Placing her hands on J.D.'s warm chest, Katherine
kneaded the rough hair with her fingers. Silently she lifted
her lips to brush his rough jawline, tasting his skin with the
tip of her tongue.

Breathing quietly, J.D. closed his eyes; Katherine instantly took the advantage and moved closer.

She needed the security of his arms when she opened her
heart. "I never told Big Jim I loved him," she whispered
shakily, then continued, "...in the way that I feel about
you."

His arms tightened possessively around her and a shudder ran the length of his tense body. "That's news," he
rasped. Then Katherine knew she had to move on, had to
sweep him off his feet. In the tomorrows she'd tell him what
he still wanted to know.

Placing her face against his throat, she nuzzled his body,
savoring its warm, masculine scent. His pulse beat rapidly

beneath her cheek, his body was tense beneath her hands as her palms skimmed around to his back.

Tracing its width and strength, Katherine slipped her finger into the waistline of his briefs and tugged slightly.

"Can two play this game?" he asked roughly, breathing in the fragrance of her hair.

Against his lips she whispered, "It's no game, darling. I'm playing for real."

He caught her bottom lip with his teeth, nibbling gently. "So am I."

Trailing her finger across his mouth, Katherine whispered, "I love you." The words were new and lingered on her tongue; she knew she would be saying them again in the tomorrows.

"It's been a long time coming," he muttered, watching her as though he would never forget the way she looked. He turned to kiss the center of her palm in a silent promise.

Lifting her into his arms, J.D. carried her to the bed. The gesture was purely pagan—a ceremonial rite, she realized in some remote corner of her brain—just as she became aware that her body was naked and hot against his.

Laying her on the satin comforter, J.D. slid a shaking hand down the length of her body from shoulder to toe, claiming her.

Then came the sound of the wind howling around the cottage, images of flames—and their bodies blending in the mirrors.

Hunger raced between them, catching, feeding, building, wanting to be satisfied.

Then there was no more time for promises.

His heart raced against hers; her breasts blended softly with the male hardness that was flattening them. Silky skin glided against rougher texture, mouths met and drank sweetness from each other.

In all the wildness there was cherishing, and promises were given.

Running his hands through her hair, J.D. sifted the glistening strands through his fingers. His kisses made her ache, built the heat as his palms cupped her breasts, kneading the softness.

Rising, she urged him with her hips to take....

Her hair flowed across his skin, silver on bronze. Its scent clung to him, entwining him more firmly in her spell.

Heat throbbed through her like a furnace, and the first wave made her tense as she sought to hold the pleasure within. Moving her hand downward, she held him until the throbbing crested, then guided him within her.

"Oh, Kat," he said roughly against her breast. "I love you."

His mouth, warm and moist, opened onto her breast and a jolt of white-hot need coursed through her body. Binding him to herself, Katherine followed where he led, then led as he followed.

She surged against his strength as she knew she would for years, first fighting, then accepting him and taking him to her heart.

There in the tangle of sheets and limbs and dancing flames she gave her life to him. J.D. met her on another plane, and the aching void closed softly within her.

Afterward, J.D. rested his head on the pillow with hers, his body keeping hers warm.

She stroked his damp shoulders and soothed the tense muscles. She liked tending him, caring for him. As she kissed his temple, she too felt at ease under his lazy hands.

Their toes mingled and played in a small gesture that cherished.

Shifting his weight, J.D. turned her toward the fire and fitted his long body to her back. He found her breast, gently taking the softness into his palm. Wrapped in each other, the sound of the wind outside and the crackling fire, they watched the dying flames together.

Katherine snuggled against him. Kissing the side of her throat, J.D. murmured, "I love you."

Arching her back against the strong body that cradled hers as if she were a sleek cat, Katherine turned to meet his sweet, lingering kiss. "Say it again," she demanded softly. "A third time makes it true."

Smiling, he obeyed. Feeling drowsy and very loved, Katherine skimmed her hand down his hard thigh while the flames danced and sputtered, catching a bead of pitch.

She felt him move his hand over her stomach and lower, claiming her once more. Katherine was content. There was nothing like having J.D. do as she asked.

"Now you say it," she heard J.D. say into her ear. "And we'll take it from there."

Katherine had a cause. After a month of marriage, J.D. still had not admitted that she was romantic. He was withholding the statement, using it as bait, just as he had waved Irish in front of her.

Listening to his husky, shower version of "Love Me Tender," Katherine adjusted her long, black Chinese robe. A wedding gift from her husband, it was wicked to the third degree. Embroidered with dragons and flowers, the robe slithered silkily against her naked body.

She lighted the candles that were surrounded by Christmas holly and blew out the match's flame. She glanced around their mountaintop retreat which J.D. had bought because he was "damned tired of having everyone around on his honeymoon." Travis was safe in Irish's loving care, music by Mancini was coming from the tape player, and the steaks were waiting. Arriving earlier than J.D., she had spent hours dedicating herself to beauty before he came in from Denver.

Katherine lifted her wrist to test the new, sultry fragrance. It was positively sinful, just like her pedicured, painted toenails.

J.D. was a scoundrel; scoundrelling was in his bones. But this time her honor was at stake; it was a matter of pride. He was tough, forcing her to eat properly and rest, removing her from her cases in the most delightful ways.

As a result, her courtroom confidence and control were back, though she somehow still doubted her control where her husband was concerned.

She scanned the night beyond the large windows that gave a view of the rugged, snow-covered mountains. She wriggled her toes against the carpeting, tugging at it gently, just as she loved to do with the hair that covered J.D.'s chest. A harem ring, another gift from her husband, glistened on her foot.

Feeling that odd, tingly sensation at the back of her neck, Katherine leaned back into J.D.'s arm and let him nuzzle the fragrant hair at her temple. She heard him whisper, "I love you."

His large, warm palm swept inside her robe to seek her waist. Turning her against him, J.D. eased her softness to his hard chest and closed his eyes. Katherine placed her arms around his neck and kissed the length of his lashes. He had that pleased look about him, as though he knew he had a surprise coming and she was it. It was an expression that often helped her overcome his nasty mood before his morning coffee—and his tyrannical demands when he had a cold.

Respect between them grew daily, nourished and cherished by both.

Travis added himself to the circle, and Katherine found herself looking at the prospect of having J.D.'s child. After visiting her doctor and finding that without protection, pregnancy could occur easily, she had dreamed for days.

Moving her parted lips softly around his mouth, Katherine presented her case for love.

"Now this is worth waiting for," he drawled, finding her lips. "Tell me," he demanded huskily.

"I love you, darling." She said the words and meant them, watching him absorb their flavor and depth.

When she hesitated, he opened one eye. "But what?"

Katherine caressed his lean cheeks with her fingertips, tracing the hard outline. He opened his other eye then narrowed it. "You're up to something, Kat."

"Am I?" she asked sweetly, moving against him. J.D. had penalties to pay for making her see how much she needed him in her life. Loving was the crime. He'd been judged and found guilty.

She walked her fingers up his chest, looking at him beneath her lashes. "Don't you think it's time we talked about signing Irish's debts over to me?"

Smiling sexily, he caressed her back. "Not a chance. But I'm open to review any bait you might have—"

Katherine showed him. And along the way he'd admit she was romantic, of course.

* * * * *

Silhouette Special Edition

Appearing in October
for a return engagement, Nora Roberts's
bestselling 1988 miniseries featuring

THE O'HURLEYS!
Nora Roberts

Book 1   **THE LAST HONEST WOMAN**   *Abby's Story*
Book 2   **DANCE TO THE PIPER**   *Maddy's Story*
Book 3   **SKIN DEEP**   *Chantel's Story*

And making his debut in a brand-new title, a very special
leading man . . . Trace O'Hurley!

Book 4   **WITHOUT A TRACE**   *Trace's Tale*

In 1988, Nora Roberts introduced THE O'HURLEYS!—a close-knit
family of entertainers whose early travels spanned the country. The
beautiful triplet sisters and their mysterious brother each experience
the triumphant joy and passion only true love can bring, in four books
you will remember long after the last pages are turned.

Don't miss this captivating miniseries in October—a special collector's edition available wherever paperbacks are sold.

OHUR-1

Double your reading pleasure this fall with two Award of Excellence titles written by two of your favorite authors.

Available in September

DUNCAN'S BRIDE
by Linda Howard
Silhouette Intimate Moments #349

Mail-order bride Madelyn Patterson was nothing like what Reese Duncan expected—and everything he needed.

Available in October

THE COWBOY'S LADY
by Debbie Macomber
Silhouette Special Edition #626

The Montana cowboy wanted a little lady at his beck and call—the "lady" in question saw things differently....

These titles have been selected to receive a special laurel—the Award of Excellence. Look for the distinctive emblem on the cover. It lets you know there's something truly wonderful inside! DUN-1

Take 4 bestselling love stories FREE

Plus get a FREE surprise gift!

Special Limited-time Offer

Silhouette Reader Service®

Mail to
In the U.S.
3010 Walden Avenue
P.O. Box 1867
Buffalo, N.Y. 14269-1867

In Canada
P.O. Box 609
Fort Erie, Ontario
L2A 5X3

YES! Please send me 4 free Silhouette Desire® novels and my free surprise gift. Then send me 6 brand-new novels every month, which I will receive months before they appear in bookstores. Bill me at the low price of $2.24* each—a savings of 26¢ apiece off cover prices. There are no shipping, handling or other hidden costs. I understand that accepting the books and gift places me under no obligation ever to buy any books. I can always return a shipment and cancel at any time. Even if I never buy another book from Silhouette, the 4 free books and the surprise gift are mine to keep forever.

*Offer slightly different in Canada—$2.24 per book plus 69¢ per shipment for delivery. Sales tax applicable in N.Y.

326 BPA 8177   (CAM)

225 BPA JAZP (US)

Name _____ (PLEASE PRINT)

Address _____ Apt. No. _____

City _____ State/Prov. _____ Zip/Postal Code _____

This offer is limited to one order per household and not valid to present Silhouette Desire® subscribers. Terms and prices are subject to change.

© 1990 Harlequin Enterprises Limited

PASSPORT TO ROMANCE
SWEEPSTAKES RULES

1 **HOW TO ENTER:** To enter, you must be the age of majority and complete the official entry form, or print your name, address, telephone number and age on a plain piece of paper and mail to: Passport to Romance, P.O. Box 9056, Buffalo, NY 14269-9056. No mechanically reproduced entries accepted.

2 All entries must be received by the CONTEST CLOSING DATE, DECEMBER 31, 1990 TO BE ELIGIBLE.

3 **THE PRIZES:** There will be ten (10) Grand Prizes awarded, each consisting of a choice of a trip for two people from the following list:
   i) London, England (approximate retail value $5,050 U.S.)
   ii) England, Wales and Scotland (approximate retail value $6,400 U.S.)
   iii) Carribean Cruise (approximate retail value $7,300 U.S.)
   iv) Hawaii (approximate retail value $9,550 U.S.)
   v) Greek Island Cruise in the Mediterranean (approximate retail value $12,250 U.S.)
   vi) France (approximate retail value $7,300 U.S.)

4 Any winner may choose to receive any trip or a cash alternative prize of $5,000.00 U.S. in lieu of the trip.

5 **GENERAL RULES:** Odds of winning depend on number of entries received.

6 A random draw will be made by Nielsen Promotion Services, an independent judging organization, on January 29, 1991, in Buffalo, NY, at 11:30 a.m. from all eligible entries received on or before the Contest Closing Date.

7 Any Canadian entrants who are selected must correctly answer a time-limited, mathematical skill-testing question in order to win.

8 Full contest rules may be obtained by sending a stamped, self-addressed envelope to: "Passport to Romance Rules Request", P.O. Box 9998, Saint John, New Brunswick, Canada E2L 4N4.

9 Quebec residents may submit any litigation respecting the conduct and awarding of a prize in this contest to the Régie des loteries et courses du Québec.

10 Payment of taxes other than air and hotel taxes is the sole responsibility of the winner.

11 Void where prohibited by law.

COUPON BOOKLET OFFER TERMS

To receive your Free travel-savings coupon booklets, complete the mail-in Offer Certificate on the preceeding page, including the necessary number of proofs-of-purchase, and mail to: Passport to Romance, P.O. Box 9057, Buffalo, NY 14269-9057. The coupon booklets include savings on travel-related products such as car rentals, hotels, cruises, flowers and restaurants. Some restrictions apply. The offer is available in the United States and Canada. Requests must be postmarked by January 25, 1991. Only proofs-of-purchase from specially marked "Passport to Romance" Harlequin® or Silhouette® books will be accepted. The offer certificate must accompany your request and may not be reproduced in any manner. Offer void where prohibited or restricted by law. LIMIT FOUR COUPON BOOKLETS PER NAME, FAMILY, GROUP, ORGANIZATION OR ADDRESS. Please allow up to 8 weeks after receipt of order for shipment. Enter quickly as quantities are limited. Unfulfilled mail-in offer requests will receive free Harlequin® or Silhouette® books (not previously available in retail stores), in quantities equal to the number of proofs-of-purchase required for Levels One to Four, as applicable.

OFFICIAL SWEEPSTAKES ENTRY FORM

Complete and return this Entry Form immediately—the more Entry Forms you submit, the better your chances of winning!
- Entry Forms must be received by **December 31, 1990**
- A random draw will take place on **January 29, 1991**
- Trip must be taken by **December 31, 1991**

3-SD-1-SW

YES, I want to win a PASSPORT TO ROMANCE vacation for two! I understand the prize includes round-trip air fare, accommodation and a daily spending allowance.

Name_____

Address_____

City_____ State_____ Zip_____

Telephone Number_____ Age_____

Return entries to: **PASSPORT TO ROMANCE**, P.O. Box 9056, Buffalo, NY 14269-9056

© 1990 Harlequin Enterprises Limited

COUPON BOOKLET/OFFER CERTIFICATE

Item	LEVEL ONE Booklet 1	LEVEL TWO Booklet 1 & 2	LEVEL THREE Booklet 1, 2 & 3	LEVEL FOUR Booklet 1, 2, 3 & 4
Booklet 1 = $100+	$100+	$100+	$100+	$100+
Booklet 2 = $200+		$200+	$200+	$200+
Booklet 3 = $300+			$300+	$300+
Booklet 4 = $400+				$400+
Approximate Total Value of Savings	$100+	$300+	$600+	$1,000+
# of Proofs of Purchase Required	4	6	12	18
Check One				

Name_____

Address_____

City_____ State_____ Zip_____

Return Offer Certificates to: **PASSPORT TO ROMANCE**, P.O. Box 9057, Buffalo, NY 14269-9057

Requests must be postmarked by **January 25, 1991**

ONE PROOF OF PURCHASE

3-SD-1

To collect your free coupon booklet you must include the necessary number of proofs-of-purchase with a properly completed Offer Certificate

© 1990 Harlequin Enterprises Limited

See previous page for details.